He lay in bed in a room much grander than any he had ever seen before.

His eyes were so swollen, he could only view the room around him as though seeing through a chink in a wall. Then he remembered the beautiful young woman who had saved him from the well and brought him in here.

Where was she?

Turning his head, he saw her standing by the window, gazing out. He had never seen so exquisite a young woman. And when she'd spoken to him in the well her voice was like honey or velvet or a warm Louisiana sunset.

Would a creature so elegant ever look fondly on him? Was it too impossible to consider? Back home the girls had liked him but they were not like this, so fine and lovely.

As he lay there gazing at her with half-closed eyes, he knew he wanted her love more than he'd ever desired anything else in his life.

Once upon a Time

WATER SONG

A Retelling of "The Frog Prince"

BY SUZANNE WEYN

SIMON PULSE
New York   London   Toronto   Sydney

This book is a work of fiction. Any references to historical events, real people, or real locales are used fictitiously. Other names, characters, places, and incidents are the product of the author's imagination, and any resemblance to actual events or locales or persons, living or dead, is entirely coincidental.

SIMON PULSE

An imprint of Simon & Schuster Children's Publishing Division

1230 Avenue of the Americas, New York, NY 10020

Copyright © 2006 by Suzanne Weyn

All rights reserved, including the right of reproduction in whole or in part in any form.

SIMON PULSE and colophon are registered trademarks of Simon & Schuster, Inc.

Designed by Karin Paprocki

The text of this book was set in Adobe Jenson.

Manufactured in the United States of America

First Simon Pulse edition October 2006

2 4 6 8 10 9 7 5 3 1

Library of Congress Control Number 2006927340

ISBN-13: 978-1-4424-6052-2

"Why am I crying? I'll tell you. My golden ball fell down the well, and I've lost it now forever."

"I will help you," said the frog. "But what will you give me if I bring back your plaything?"

—"The Frog Prince," by the Brothers
Grimm, as retold by Naomi Lewis

". . . British forces continued to push the Germans back a few hundred yards at a time toward the high ridge at Passchendaele. The Germans fought back with mustard gas, a notoriously slow-acting chemical agent that maimed or killed enemy soldiers via severe blisters on the skin or internally if breathed. . . . The British reached Passchendaele on October 12 during a driving rain that turned the landscape to impenetrable mud."

—World War I, History SparkNotes

Breathe. Just breathe.

—"Breathe (2 AM)," Anna Nalick

PROLOGUE
Belgium, April 1915

"What a fool I was!" Emma Winthrop muttered, furious at herself as she stared down at Lloyd Pennington's handsome face in the photo in her opened locket. She sat on a stone wall outside her family's estate with the two halves of the locket open in her hand. When the locket lay open like it did now, it resembled an orange that had been cut in two with its halves side by side. When closed, it was a perfect golden ball worn on a slender gold chain.

She had taken this photograph of him herself and placed it inside her locket. At the time, it had seemed wildly sophisticated to carry a picture of a good-looking boyfriend—one she'd often sneaked out to meet after dark. Back at the Hampshire Girls' Boarding School she used to kiss the photo of Lloyd each night before shutting off her lamp in the dormitory room she shared with four other girls.

The locket had originally belonged to her

great-great-grandmother and had been handed down to her great-grandmother and then to her grandmother and to her mother, who had given it to her. Sometimes it annoyed her when she slept, its round surface digging into her chest, but not even that could compel her to remove it. Back then she'd wanted Lloyd's picture beside her heart at every moment.

How she'd missed him! Dreamed of the day they would be together again. All these months the thought of him had been her only consolation.

And then, yesterday, she'd received a letter from him. A farmer friend of Claudine, the housekeeper, had brought it by. Mail was so rare these days. Hardly any got through enemy lines. She hadn't received word from anyone back in London for nearly five months.

Trembling, nearly weeping tears of joy, she'd ripped the letter open.

But his words slowly filled her with stunned coldness. He'd said that rumors were spreading that her mother had run away from her father, had gone home to her family estate, taking Emma along with her. It was causing quite the scandal in their social circle. No one expected this shocking news from such a socially prominent and respectable family. As a result, his own parents had strongly expressed their wishes that he break off his relationship with Emma. While this pained him, he understood their point. He had to think of his parents and their place in society. He had to consider his future law career and his possible political future, as well.

Finally, he got to his point: It was perhaps better if they didn't see each other anymore.

He apologized for telling her this in a letter. He'd have preferred to tell her in person, but since she was now right on the Western Front of the Great War he hadn't any idea when she planned on returning.

In conclusion, he hoped Emma would understand. It was regrettable, but one had to be realistic and deal with society on its own terms. It was the way of the world, after all.

She remembered his words as she continued gazing down at his photo. How she'd adored him! Now she couldn't stand to see Lloyd smirking at her for one more second! The smile she'd once found so irresistibly attractive now seemed merely smug and self-satisfied.

She swore under her breath in French, a habit she'd picked up in the girls' dormitory at the Hampshire School. "You imbecile!" she snarled at his picture. "My mother hasn't run away. She hasn't returned home because she's dead!"

Snapping the two halves of the golden ball shut, Emma hopped from the wall and strode purposefully to the old stone well several yards away. "To hell with you, Lloyd Pennington, you lying two-face!" she shouted as she hurled the locket. She'd always had a strong throwing arm and acute aim. As intended, the locket sailed into the well.

CHAPTER ONE
The Glowing Green Sky

Emma looked up sharply when the German plane appeared. The sunset of pink and gold filtering into the room had drawn her to the high, arched window. The brilliant quality of the light, so vibrant and yet still, poised between day and night, filled her with a quiet sadness.

But the unexpected appearance of the plane jolted her from her melancholy, diverting her into a state of hyperattentiveness.

Sometimes a lone plane like this was only spying on the Allied troops, reporting back their numbers and position in the field. At least that was what she'd read in the newspapers. In minutes, though, another plane appeared over the rolling fields below, first as a dot in the sky and then slowly coming into clearer focus. She could just barely make out the high whine of the planes' propellers.

Two planes was not a good sign. It meant they

were bombers, not reconnaissance planes. These fighter planes always showed up first, and the strategy seemed to be to bomb from above before attacking with ground troops.

Emma sighed bitterly. It was amazing how much she'd learned about war these last few months. Back at the Hampshire School when she had studied art, music, mathematics, English literature, German, French, and Latin, she'd never have suspected that months later she would become a student of war.

Nothing was more important than war now. In fact, everything else seemed almost ridiculously irrelevant. Back in London she'd pored over the papers, which were full of the war—troop locations; whether they were winning or losing; what nations had joined the fight.

In Belgium she'd learned about war firsthand, seen much more than she'd ever expected or wanted to know. She'd seen things she longed to forget.

Had her parents really thought the Great War wouldn't touch them; that she and her mother could safely visit their family estate in Belgium? How shortsighted that decision now seemed; though back in early September of 1914, her father had been certain all the fighting would be concentrated on the Russian border—the Eastern Front—and Belgium's neutrality would be respected.

He couldn't have been more wrong.

The insectlike buzz of the plane grew louder. Surely they weren't going to bombard the village of

Ypres again. What could possibly be left there that hadn't already been blasted into rubble?

Lately she drifted from one empty day to another here in the huge, rambling estate with only old Claudine and Willem, the manor's caretaker couple, there to help her. Thank god they'd stayed on. If they'd left, Emma knew she wouldn't have been able to cope at all.

She'd been stuck there for nearly seven months, since last September. The seventeenth-century manor house sat right on the line between the Allied French, English, Dutch, Canadian, and Belgian troops and the enemy, the Austrians and Germans. Both sides had dug in to filthy trenches on either side of the fighting. She was right on what had come to be known as the Western Front of the Great War.

The mansion sat on several miles of elevated cliff known as The Ridge. It gave her a perfect view of the trench-torn fields below. It was just like her to be stuck in the thick of things, right smack in the middle of trouble. Only, unlike the schoolgirl mischief she'd gotten into back at the Hampshire School, this was a mess to end all messes—a disaster on a worldwide scale. Some people said it was the end of the world.

It *felt* like the end of the world.

She and her mother should have gone home right away, but then a week later, the German hydrogen vessels, the zeppelins, flew over England and dropped missiles. No one had expected that!

Her father sent a telegram saying it might be

better to stay where they were for the moment. But they'd waited too long. Now a fight had begun to control the North Sea, and the English Channel wasn't safe to cross. The Germans had declared any vessel in those waters fair game for attack. Besides that, she couldn't get past enemy lines in the north.

If only her mother were still there with her.

Rose Winthrop had been too near a missile that exploded in Ypres during an assault on the medieval city. They'd been in a restaurant having lunch. The owner pulled the shutters closed and barricaded the door when the attack began, but the blast tore open the entire front of the restaurant. Emma had desperately mopped blood from her mother's brow and watched the once vibrant eyes grow dull as she slipped away.

It infuriated her to think that people thought her mother had run off, had abandoned her father. It was awful! Why didn't her father set the ugly rumors straight? Hadn't he told people that she had been killed?

It suddenly struck her that maybe he didn't know! Her mother had been buried outside of Ypres. Emma had written her father a letter, telling him what had happened; but maybe he'd never gotten it. She hadn't received a letter back from him in all this time. She'd assumed it was because they couldn't get letters across the enemy lines. It had never occurred to her until that moment that her letter to him had not made it to London.

A knot twisted in her stomach. Did her father think she and her mother had abandoned him? Was that why no one had come to get her?

In the beginning, right after her mother's death, she'd spent every day expecting her father to show up, to console her, to take her home. But he never came. No one came. She hadn't known what to think of this but she'd imagined every possible scenario: her father getting the news and dropping dead of a heart attack; England being attacked and her father taken prisoner; her father being killed in another missile attack. Her imagination spun out endless reasons why he had not come. Most likely, he couldn't get through to her just as she couldn't get to him, but it still didn't stop her from imagining the worst.

This letter from Lloyd meant that her father was alive but not telling anyone that her mother was dead, leaving them to think that she—and Emma—had run off and left him. Was it truly what he thought had happened? If so, how could he think that of them? Her mother would never do that—her loving, good mother—never!

Thinking of her mother made Emma's eyes well with tears. It was so senseless! So stupid! Her mother had died for no reason! Her mother had always been the one she could count on to understand her feelings; the one ready with a hug and comforting words. It was her mother to whom she'd always confided. How she missed talking with her.

And though her mother would have been her

first choice, it would have been a pleasure to have *anyone* at all to talk to these days! Willem and Claudine only spoke Flemish. And, although the sounds of Flemish were a bit like French—and somewhat like Dutch, which was likewise akin, in some ways, to German—she found it nearly impossible to communicate with the couple. Many Belgians spoke German, French, or English. Emma was fluent in all three, having excelled in language at school. Her own mother had been able to speak German and Dutch, being raised as a girl here in the manor. But with Claudine and Willem, it was Flemish or nothing, and so it was nothing.

The rattle of the first round of shelling drew Emma's thoughts back to the planes. Two more fighter planes had joined them, their red and white cross insignias just barely visible from her window.

Her hands flew to her ears, covering them against a sudden deafening blast. The nearest field erupted in white light, shot through with dirt and debris. Even from up here on The Ridge, back a safe distance from the fighting, her window rattled slightly with the impact. The shells were raining down fast now. It always began with a whistle, like ascending fireworks, and then the jarring, bone-rattling explosion. Though she'd heard it before, she could never get used to it.

Staring hard, she tried to see into the trenches out there in the fields. She couldn't detect movement in the long ditches dug into the dirt, but that didn't mean soldiers weren't there, hunkered against the dirt walls, gripping their machine guns, hand grenades, and pistols; waiting, tensely white-knuckled, for the other side to stand and advance first, foolishly exposing itself to their gunfire.

Another shell hit the ground, spraying up more blinding light and deadly debris.

Emma turned away from the window, her face tight with the effort of keeping tears at bay. How much longer could this madness continue?

So many people had died already. Her mother's death loomed larger than all the others to her, but she knew that every death was monumental to someone; every soldier a friend, boyfriend, husband, father, brother, or son. Every civilian and soldier killed was someone's dear one and an irreplaceable loss to that person. And yet the killing went on and on. The death tolls reported in the papers were staggering.

Madness! she thought again. If she heard one more shell fall she might lose her mind altogether.

She crossed the large master bedroom that had once been used by her parents. She'd moved into it because her own bedroom had a leak when it rained and it had been a rainy spring.

The four curved posts of her parents' mahogany bed nearly reached the top of the ceiling. A maroon-colored brocade cloth was draped from post to post. The matching bedcover lay rumpled across the unmade bed.

Emma crawled into it, kicking aside the knotted sheet before pulling her legs into a fetal crouch. Her tears flowed freely now into her pillow, until she had sobbed her way into the relief of sleep.

She dreamed she was having tea with the girls in her dormitory. They sat downstairs in the school's parlor, so happy to be back in the familiar safety of the school once again, back among friends. They were gossiping about someone. She heard their words but couldn't make sense of them. "Who are you talking about?" she asked.

"Don't you know?" asked a girl named Theresa. "It's that Rose Winthrop. She ran away from her husband and then she abandoned her daughter in Europe somewhere—just dumped her and ran off with some man."

"She did not!" Emma objected angrily.

Theresa and the others giggled knowingly. "Yes, she did, silly. Everyone in England knows about it," a second girl named Augusta insisted. "Mr. Winthrop has disowned the mother *and* the daughter, both. He wants nothing to do with either one of them. He has forgotten them entirely and has begun a new family."

"He has not!" Emma screamed, red-faced with humiliation and outrage. "Stop saying that! Stop it!"

She sat straight up in bed, wide awake once again and realizing she'd shouted out loud.

The rapid staccato of machine gun fire now filled the blank spaces between the bombings from above. But something new was happening, something she had never seen before. She noticed it the moment she gazed toward the window.

Swinging her legs out of bed, she returned to the window for a closer look.

Out in the fields, a sickly, greenish-yellow vapor came rising up from the ground. It was like no color she'd ever seen before.

What *was* it?

The ghostly mist seemed strangely evil and filled Emma with an icy dread.

For a moment, both the bombing and the machine gun fire ceased. Her ears adjusted to the sudden silence and she became aware of another sound.

She wasn't certain . . . but . . .

She thought she heard a voice . . . no.

It was many voices.

And they were screaming.

CHAPTER TWO
Fire in His Lungs

Jack Verde was on fire. He felt as if someone had blasted a blowtorch straight into his eyes. He'd gotten to his knees and sucked in a last gasp of good air when he saw others around him start to choke.

He'd done it just in time too, because the gas, apparently heavier than the air, was quickly sinking down and settling into the trenches. He knew this because the green glowed most intensely closest to the ground.

Blindly he groped his way out of the muddy earthworks of the trench, desperate to escape the deadly mist. On every side, other soldiers did the same but he could only see them as dim outlines.

The only thing real to him was the drive to get away from the foul and burning air.

A hand gripped him. "Jack! Help!"

He recognized the voice immediately and pulled

a large handkerchief from his uniform pocket, thrusting it toward the young soldier's face, pressing it over his mouth and nose. He didn't dare speak or he'd lose the gulp of air he'd managed to inhale before the poison gas enveloped them completely.

He gestured for the soldier, who was no more than a boy, to follow him out of the trench. Before they had gone a yard, though, a shell exploded several feet away.

The boy flew into the air, thrown by the impact. All around him, soldiers were upended.

As the debris rained down in the thick, acrid fog, he searched for the boy, going back into the trench and following it for several yards.

He couldn't find him. Hopefully he'd been able to make a run for it, just as all the others were now doing.

Jack climbed above the trench again, his arms out, stumbling blindly forward. His fogged vision produced only dark outlines of fleeing men.

Still holding his breath, he kept moving ahead, not knowing what else to do. He didn't dare shut his burning eyes for fear of stumbling into a roll of barbed wire. If he became entangled in its lethal spikes it would be the end of him.

He'd been staring at this open field from the protection of the trench for days now. Of all times to get stuck here with this French regiment! Because he spoke French, he and the kid soldier had been sent to deliver a message from their own English and Canadian unit farther north. But the Germans had moved in unexpectedly and cut them off, leaving them stranded there.

Sitting in the filthy, rat-infested trench with nothing to do but look out had burned the landscape into his memory. The fields rolled on for miles before ending in a distant ridge with some impressive, manor-type structure sitting on top of it. In the distance, maybe two miles away or so, were trees. If he could get to the shelter of the trees, maybe they would shield him from the poison.

Several yards out, he marveled that he had still not been caught by a grenade, stumbled into a shell hole, or been snagged on barbed wire. He was in a crowd of fleeing soldiers, yet they could do nothing to help one another. Each of them suffered in his own private hell.

His lungs strained, screaming for oxygen. He held on longer, knowing he had to make use of what air he had. He, who could hold his breath longer than anyone else he knew; the champion of underwater swimming—he had to hold on now as if his life depended on it.

His life did depend on it.

A searing pain on his arm made him glance sharply at his uniform sleeve, checking for fire. He saw no flame, but his flesh continued to burn. The cloth must be absorbing the poison gas.

Frantically he began to strip off his jacket. The burning spread, as if he was spreading it by moving the cloth. He couldn't get the uniform off fast enough.

He clutched at the straps and buckles of his boots, yanking them off, tossing them blindly. He wasted no time in climbing out of his putty-colored leggings. The burning lessened, but there must still be some chemical in his tan union suit, the army-issued, one-piece undergarment he still wore. He began to tear at the tiny buttons, unable to unbutton them fast enough. Before he could get his union suit off, he teetered forward and tripped over a spent shell casing, hurtling onto the dirt.

His breath was knocked out sharply. As he instinctively inhaled, the scorching pain ran up his nostrils, down his throat, and traveled straight into his lungs.

His lungs fought to expel the invisible inferno raging within them. He collapsed into a fit of uncontrollable coughing, feeling consciousness lift and leave him, when suddenly . . .

He was swimming under the cool, lovely water. He was swimming in the Mississippi River.

He was free.

Free from the police who were going to take him for a crime he didn't commit. He'd never again see the inside of the waif's home where he'd spent the end of his boyhood. He would miss the jazz of New Orleans, but that was all right. The current was carrying him away to a new life.

All the magic his mother had taught him before her death would serve him in this new adventure. Every trick he'd learned in order to survive on his own on Bourbon Street would come in handy now.

He stopped swimming and popped his head above the surface for air. . . .

And he awoke once again into the cloud of putrid green air. And he knew that now, as then, water was the only thing that could save him.

Chapter Three
In the Well

The next morning, Emma stepped out of the manor into the cool, dewy morning and almost immediately she coughed. Her eyes and her throat tingled. Was the sickly green mist from the night before still lingering in the air? Were the spring breezes now blowing it her way?

She considered going back inside. It would be the smart thing to do if something unhealthy lingered in the air. Wiping her eyes, she convinced herself she had no more than a touch of hay fever.

The dream she'd had of the girls gossiping about her parents had made her long for them more than ever. With the bombs falling outside her window, she desperately wished to see them and had remembered that she had a photo of them in her locket. She'd put the picture of Lloyd over it, but it would still be there and . . .

That was when she realized—with a slowly spreading chill—what she'd done. She had rashly hurled her locket into the well, forgetting all about the photo of her parents that lay beneath Lloyd's photograph.

And not only had she lost the picture of her parents, she'd also lost a family heirloom that had been in her family for over a century. She pictured the locket now, as it had been when she held it in her hand the day before. One half of the sphere contained a glass-covered frame suitable for inserting a picture—the place where she'd put Lloyd's picture over that of her parents. The other half had a compartment that didn't open although, if shaken, something clearly rattled around inside it.

Her mother had told her she didn't know what the sealed half held. "Great-grandmother said it was a little something for an emergency and that I should be content to leave it there in case one should arise," her mother had revealed. "I hope you'll never need to know what it is."

Upon receiving it, Emma had burned with curiosity, attempting to pry it loose with her fingernails, toothpicks, kitchen knives; but nothing worked. Often she would shake it wondering what it could be. A poison capsule? A priceless jewel? A secret code revealing that she was related to the queen?

How could she have thrown it down the well? "I am such a total idiot!" she blamed herself, throwing her arms out from her sides in frustration as she moved toward the well.

In her anger at Lloyd she hadn't stopped to remember that her mother's picture was under there. The last night's nearby attack had reawakened all her dread of the war and her terror at being left here on her own. She felt desperate to see her parents' faces once again! If she didn't make it back to London, it might be her last chance to ever look at them again. She suddenly felt desperate to see her mother's face once more.

How beautiful her mother had been with her wavy, auburn hair so like Emma's, and with the same gray-blue eyes. That's where their similarity ended, though. Emma had none of her mother's fragility or delicate grace; at least she couldn't see it in herself.

There were, though, less visible things that she'd gotten from her mother, such as her impulsive temperament. Hadn't her mother recklessly run off to Belgium saying she was worried about her family's ancestral home and felt an urgent need to check on it? And hadn't Emma insisted just as impulsively on going with her, bored with the rounds of society parties and eager for a more interesting adventure?

And now in one burst of frustration, an ill-considered fit of pique, she'd thrown away her only picture of her parents, not to mention the golden locket itself, and whatever emergency valuable was stashed in the other half.

Peering over the side of the well into the darkness below, she wondered if she could get it back somehow. It wasn't the North Sea or even the English Channel, after all. It was only a well.

Checking around, she looked for Willem. The old caretaker was never there when she needed him! Of course, she couldn't ask the ancient old troll to climb down the well, but at least he might help her with the very tall ladder she'd seen leaning up against the garden shed at the back of the estate the other day.

Checking for the ladder, she saw that it was no longer there. Strange. What could Willem be doing with such a tall ladder? Surely he was too frail to climb it.

She just had to get that locket back!

With a sigh, she planted her hands on her hips and considered the well. No longer in use, it had long ago lost its protective roof and windup bucket. It was actually just a deep stone pit in the ground and probably should be covered up. She made a mental note to tell Willem to board it over.

Was there even water in it?

Unsure, she went to the well and leaned over its wall as far as she could and peered into the darkness below. Very far down, a small circle of sunlight was reflected back to her, proving that there was indeed water inside.

But was the circle really sunlight, or the ball medallion of her locket?

Digging her nails into the crevices of the stones for support, she leaned in farther. Then, for the first time, she saw that the tall ladder was inside the well leaning against its inside wall.

It was definitely the same ladder she'd seen the

other day. This meant that since yesterday, someone had dropped it down into the well. She doubted that Willem could have managed it. But then who did?

When her eyes had adjusted somewhat to the darkness within the well, she became aware of an even darker mass at the bottom. It splashed. An animal, perhaps? It could have been panicked by yesterday's bombing and stumbled in. Tilting her head for a better angle, she tried to make out its shape. Whatever it was, it was large.

Emma shifted her grip on the well's wall and knocked a stone down into the well. Before plunking into the water with the unmistakable sound of a wet surface being broken, it first hit the solid mass, causing the creature to cough as though it were trying to rid itself of its very lungs—and might soon succeed.

Emma knew instantly that this was no animal.

There was a man at the bottom of her well.

CHAPTER FOUR
Trapped

Three quarters of the way down the ladder, Emma's bare foot hit cold water. "Hello?" she called, peering into the black water and just barely making out his shoulders and head against the cylindrical wall. The rest of him was submerged below the surface. He had to be freezing!

"Are you all right?" she asked mildly. *Stupid question,* she chided herself. *Of course he's not all right!* She hiked up her ankle-length skirt, tucking its hem into her waistband to keep it dry as she stood on the ladder, knee-deep in water.

He could only cough in reply.

As her eyes adjusted further to the darkness, she could almost make out his appearance. He was young, maybe a little older than she, with close-cropped black hair. At first she thought he wore no shirt but then realized that some sort of plain, collarless tan cloth was plastered to his soaked body.

But she couldn't make out his eyes. Something was wrong with them. What?

He made no move toward her but turned his face away, still coughing, trying hard to stop, his hand raised to support himself against the well's wall, his shoulders heaving with the effort.

"Come on," she said. "Let's get you out of here."

He turned and stepped forward into the patch of sunlight. She cringed to see his eyes. They were swollen nearly shut, the lids puffed to three times the size they should have been.

And his skin was peeling, almost in shreds at some spots!

He looked to her like some sort of a giant amphibian. Yes, a frog, with his mottled skin and bulging, slitted eyes, was croaking there in the water.

She shoved the thought aside as being uncharitable and was instantly ashamed. He was injured, after all. He couldn't help how he looked. She realized he was most probably a soldier.

"Do you speak German?" she asked, speaking in German she had studied in school.

He stepped back against the wall.

"English?" she asked in English.

"Eng . . . I'm with the English . . . ," he managed in a rasp before the coughing overtook him once again.

His accent surprised her. "You're American," she surmised.

He nodded as he coughed, leaning against the well's wall.

Had the Americans declared war? She hadn't heard that they had joined the fight, though the Allied Forces desperately hoped they would. They needed American soldiers to replace their injured and war-weary troops, as well as American supplies to replenish their depleted resources.

At least he wasn't an enemy soldier, at any rate. That would have made the situation a lot more complicated.

Once his coughing finally calmed down, she extended her hand to him. "Come on. You have to get up the ladder," she said.

He pulled away from her, shaking his head violently.

"You must. You'll die if you stay down here," she insisted.

He pointed up. "Gas!"

"Gas? I don't understand," she said. "Do you mean gasoline? Did you come here in a motorcar?"

Again he shook his head, then slumped against the wall as if tired out by the effort of communicating even that much. The memory of the greenish vapor she'd seen the day before came back to Emma, and she felt sick as its meaning became clear to her.

It *was* gas, then! Poison chlorine gas!

She'd read about it in the newspapers. The Germans and Austrians had tried to use poison gas on England's allies, the Russians, on the war's Eastern Front. But it had been too cold in Russia.

The cold air had done something to the gas, making it ineffective. But apparently it had worked here, thanks to the fine, Belgian spring.

"There is no gas up there," she told him. "Well, maybe just a bit left," she said, remembering the tingling in her throat. "Most of it didn't come this far or else it's blown off. You're safe now. We have to get you some help."

She shivered as the cold water began to chill her. "We really must get out of here," she said again.

The news that there was no more gas aboveground seemed to take the panic out of him and he came toward her, sloshing through the water. "Can you climb?" she asked. "If you're strong enough, we can go slowly and you can feel your way along."

He nodded and Emma took the lead. Above them, the round opening of bright blue sky grew larger and brighter as they neared the top. From time to time she checked behind to make sure the soldier was still with her. One time, he rested his head on the rung of a ladder, seeming unable to continue, but after a moment's rest, resumed their climb.

"Nearly there," Emma encouraged him, again checking down. Turning back, she noticed that the sun had suddenly shaded over.

Looking up, she confronted two pairs of vivid blue eyes in unsmiling faces topped by the distinctive helmets of German soldiers. "The two of you! Get out of there! Now!" one of the soldiers barked in German. "Quickly—or we shoot!"

Chapter Five
Jack Sprat

Emma faced the German colonel and was surprised to discover that the situation felt oddly similar to the time she was called on the carpet before Headmistress Morris after she'd been caught sneaking back into the school after her meeting with Lloyd. Of course the headmistress hadn't been flanked by two bayonet-carrying, helmeted soldiers, but surely those cold blue eyes were just as daunting as the ones she faced at this moment.

Well, maybe not quite.

But still . . . the situation did not feel entirely unfamiliar. She did now what she had done then: She thrust her chin forward defiantly, squared her shoulders, made her eyes go steely, and, in general, did her utmost to project an image of British upper-class superiority.

"You will explain to me why you were hiding in

the well with this soldier," the colonel, a tall, blond man, demanded roughly in heavily accented English.

With a darting glance, Emma checked on the man from the well, held tightly between the two German soldiers. In the sunlight she saw that he was no frog, just a badly injured soldier in soaking, one-piece underwear.

The horrible, pointed bayonets at the ends of the soldiers' rifles gleamed in the early afternoon light. Emma's words were spoken in the excellent German she'd learned at the Hampshire School. She hadn't planned to speak them either, but they came almost on their own. The ability to quickly concoct an impromptu cover story when under pressure was a skill she'd had the chance to hone during her many mishaps at the boarding school.

"First, let me begin by saying that this is my property and I have every right to go down my well if it pleases me to do so. Second, this man is no soldier. He was out hiking yesterday and wandered into a cloud of your unspeakable gas. Look what it did to him," she scolded indignantly. "Stumbling home in pain, he fell into our open well. He spent the entire night there before I found him just now."

The German colonel looked sharply from the injured soldier and back to Emma. "Who is this man to you?" he asked in German.

"My husband," Emma replied with the first lie that sprang to her lips.

"I see no wedding ring," the colonel snapped,

making Emma wish she had said he was her brother. But that might not have worked. If they figured out that he was American, they would know it was not true.

"I sold it," she replied. "We are cut off from our home by your wretched submarines, and food is in short supply here. The farmers charge a very inflated price, but we get hungry and need to pay whatever they demand."

The colonel studied Emma. "I can tell from your accent that you are English. What about . . ." He jerked his head disdainfully toward the soldier who seemed about to collapse as he hung there between the two German soldiers. "Also English?"

"American." Since he actually was American, it seemed like a good idea to let the colonel know that. The Americans had no troops here, as far as she knew. The fact that he was American would make it more believable that he was not a soldier. "And I am American because I am his wife," she added. "I want nothing more than to wait out this war and go home with my husband to America." She hoped he would not ask her exactly where in America, since she had no idea.

"You do not think America should join the war?" the colonel inquired suspiciously.

"Absolutely not!" she replied. "Just because some Serbian lunatic shot the kaiser's cousin? It's insanity! My husband and I want our country to have no part in this war! We have even marched with the isolationists."

This last bit she took from a newspaper article she'd read recounting the widespread feeling among Americans that they wanted to stay out of the war.

He still didn't seem convinced as he strode arrogantly over to the soldier. "Tell me your name!" he demanded in English.

The soldier began to cough.

"Your name!" the colonel barked harshly.

"Jack Sprat," the soldier said, spitting out the words.

That can't be his name, Emma realized, remembering the old nursery rhyme: *Jack Sprat would eat no fat. His wife would eat no lean. But together, the two of them would lick the plate quite clean.*

The colonel did not make the connection, however, and accepted his answer, convinced by the American accent. He turned his attention back to Emma, speaking in German again. "Who owns this estate?"

"I do."

"We will be using it as a base, and my men will be garrisoned here."

"What?" Emma cried indignantly.

"This mountain ridge gives us a perfect vantage point from which to see the enemy advancing across the fields."

"But I don't want you here," Emma protested. "I won't allow it!"

The colonel laughed. "What you want doesn't matter. My men have already begun to move in. You and your husband can stay on in your chambers as our guests."

"We don't want to stay here with you," Emma insisted angrily.

"We can shoot you. Would you prefer that?" he snapped, clearly losing patience with her.

"Are we free to leave?" she dared ask, her tone chastened by the harshness that had come into his voice.

He considered this a moment. "No. I think not. You know the running of the place. We might need information from you. And I don't want you leaving to tell the enemy all about us. To be blunt: You and your husband are our prisoners. We will need your caretakers to stay, as well."

He spoke sharply to his two men. "Take them into their chambers and lock them inside."

Emma shivered as the lock bolt in the door clicked shut behind her. The soldier, her "husband," had been roughly shoved to the floor and lay there in a heap.

"Come on," she said gently, getting into a squat position and sliding her arms under his armpits. "Let's get you into the bed." She attempted to drag him but, although trim and athletic, he was remarkably solid and heavy. It took all her effort to get him next to the bed.

When she tried to lift him up into it, she found it impossible. She kept nearly lifting him onto the bed only to drop him to the floor at the last second.

"Sorry," she apologized in embarrassment the second time she bumped his head against the wooden foot of the bed.

The thump seemed to rouse him a bit, and his bulging, slitted eyes opened slightly, revealing deep brown pupils.

"Hold on there, sug," he croaked, pronouncing the endearment like the first part of the word *sugar*.

Reaching up, he gripped the foot post and pulled himself up onto the bed. He sat at the bed's edge a moment, supported by his arms, before toppling onto his back with his legs still dangling over the side.

Emma scrambled onto the bed beside him, putting her face close to his. "Can I get you anything?" she offered.

He turned so that they were face-to-face. "How about a kiss, sug?"

Emma sprang back as though a firecracker had exploded between them. "Did I hear you correctly? Did you just ask me for a kiss?"

Improbable as it looked on his battered, scorched, swollen-eyed face, a grin spread across it. "Yeah, you right, I did. How 'bout it?"

"You're disgusting!" she cried, outraged. "I just saved your life, you know! And that's how you thank me?"

"Aw c'mon, sug. Don't be that way," he said, his voice fading into a whisper. "I bet you have the sweetest kisses, and I ain't been kissed in the longest time. . . ." His last words trailed off as he shut his eyes and fell asleep.

"Well, that's certainly not surprising," Emma replied before realizing that he was asleep.

CHAPTER SIX
Bayou Magic

Jack knew he had traveled very far away. Although he had once sworn he would never return home, in this time of greatest distress, that was exactly where his spirit had instinctively come.

He sat on a large, gnarled root of a tree jutting from the murky, dark water. He was in a flooded forest of towering, bald cypress under a lush canopy alive with calling, cawing birds. Spanish moss and vines hung above him.

Was he really back in Louisiana? Was this a dream or was it real? His mam always said it didn't really matter. The dream world was a real world too. She walked through both worlds with practiced ease, which was one reason—but not the only reason—that some called her a witchy woman.

The water rippled as an alligator moved just below the surface. He watched the line it etched in the water, making sure it was going away from him rather than heading in his direction as he had done many times in his boyhood. It was never a good idea to take alligators for granted no matter how familiar you became with them.

When he stopped watching the alligator he turned to find his mother sitting on the root beside him. As she'd been in life, she was a tall, regal woman with chocolaty skin and high cheekbones, her black hair caught in a circle of braids atop her head. "You're hurt badly, son," she observed, taking his hand.

Looking down, he saw that the skin on his hands was no longer peeling. Bending forward, he gazed at his reflection in the dark water. His eyes were large, dark, and completely normal, his lips smooth and no longer blistered.

"I rose above it, like you taught me," he told her. "I jumped into the muddy ol' Mississippi and swam for my life."

She stroked his hair tenderly. "You've learned well."

"You always said I was a frog."

She laughed softly. "You are surely that, but so much more."

Reaching into the water, she pulled up a handful of thick mud. Still cupping the mud, she broke off a shelf of lichen growing on the bald cedar tree and crumpled it into a fine powder over the mud.

He flinched as she plucked two hairs from his head and stirred them into the mud and lichen powder.

He knew what she would do next and so shut his eyes to let her smear the mud across them. The cool mud soothed him as she whispered words of healing he'd often heard her murmur over the sick and wounded poor.

In their small town outside the city, where no licensed

physician ever ventured, she was no witch. There, she was a queen, the only hope the people held for release from suffering. And she never failed them.

She had learned all the ancient remedies; the ones the old people had carried with them from Haiti, from Africa, from Romania, France, and even the knowledge the native Indians brought, especially the Natchez tribe—the once great civilization from the Mississippi Valley—the great mound builders whose blood ran in her veins: It was all in her.

She came from a long line of practitioners: medicine men and women, shamans, midwives. If she could not cure an illness, she could at least relieve the suffering.

Sometimes she did this with her herbs and roots. Other times her understanding of age-old wisdoms enabled her to help the sufferer lift above and beyond the physical realm. She had chants and songs that helped her with this.

His mother placed her hands over the plaster of mud, lichen dust, and hair on his eyes. In a high, piercing voice she chanted a song she'd learned from her Natchez great-grandmother. It was a plea to the Great Spirit to restore her son's health.

When she took her hands away, she wiped off the medicine pack, tossing it into the swamp. She lifted her head, listening, as though she'd caught a faraway sound. "Your body is calling your spirit to return," she told him. "You cannot be separated from it for long. But if its pain becomes unbearable, you come back here. If I cannot make the journey, do as I did now. Cure yourself. I have taught you. You have the power. I have given you much magic."

The breeze in the trees overhead began to speed up. The cardinals and red-winged blackbirds darted among the branches in alarming swift flight. The alligator lifted its head and spread its jaws.

Clouds raced past.

It was day, then night, then day again.

He lay in bed in a room much grander than any he had ever seen before. His eyes were so swollen, he could only view the room around him as though seeing through a chink in a wall. Then he remembered the beautiful young woman who had saved him from the well and brought him in here.

Where was she?

Turning his head, he saw her standing by the window, gazing out. He had never seen so exquisite a young woman. And when she'd spoken to him in the well her voice was like honey or velvet or a warm Louisiana sunset.

Would a creature so elegant ever look fondly on him? Was it too impossible to consider? Back home the girls had liked him but they were not like this, so fine and lovely.

As he lay there gazing at her with half-closed eyes, he knew he wanted her love more than he'd ever desired anything else in his life.

CHAPTER SEVEN
Water and Escape

Emma felt deeply relieved an hour later when the door opened and white-haired, stout Claudine was unceremoniously shoved inside. In her arms she held towels and a blue ceramic bowl. The pockets of her ruffled white apron bulged with supplies from the kitchen. She cast a look of resigned misery at Emma and said something consoling in Flemish.

The kind, motherly words, although unintelligible to Emma, made unexpected tears spring to her eyes. Part of her longed for Claudine to wrap her in a hug, but that was not their relationship and Emma quickly wiped her eyes.

With a glance at the lightly snoring soldier on the bed, Claudine crossed to the small, closet-size bathroom in the back of the bedroom, an addition Emma's mother had had installed three summers past. That same summer she'd had electricity and running water installed. She'd been so excited by the improvements, saying that just because the estate was built in the 1600s, it didn't mean they had to live like they were still in the past.

Settling in next to the soldier on the bed, Claudine began to gently wipe away the grime on his face. She folded a dry hand towel and laid it over his puffed eyes, fixing it there with white surgical tape.

Emma watched Claudine tend the American while she sat curled in a large, upholstered chair. Claudine tended the soldier so efficiently, her old-woman's hands moving deftly as she stripped his clothing while keeping him covered modestly with the blanket and cleaning him without his even awakening, that Emma wondered if she'd ever been a nurse. From a tall chest of drawers, the old woman produced a pair of Emma's father's pajamas and practically swept them onto the soldier's body while he continued to slumber under the blanket.

Claudine finished by running a brush through his coarse, black hair. Putting down the brush, she stroked his forehead and spoke kind words to him in her own language. She was moving away from the bed when the soldier's hand snaked out from under the blanket and encircled her wrist.

The sudden, unexpected gesture made Emma gasp sharply, but Claudine seemed unfazed and leaned in to hear the young man better. Her hand over her thumping heart, Emma bent closer to hear.

"*Merci beaucoup, madame,*" the soldier whispered to Claudine.

A German soldier came into the room and signaled for Claudine to come with him. Emma continued to sit in the chair after Claudine departed, watching the sleeping American, his face illuminated by a patch of sunlight pouring through the window.

I wonder what he looked like before he was so injured, she thought. She really couldn't tell. Why was he fighting with the British? Surely only a very strange person would sign up to fight in a war that he didn't need to enlist in.

She thought about his request that she kiss him, and a glance at his blistered lips made her shudder at the idea. What kind of person could think of kissing while in such a state, nearly dead and a prisoner? And of kissing a woman he didn't even know, at that?

Maybe he'd been delirious or shell-shocked or something similar, she thought, softening toward him slightly for a moment. But then she threw off the charitable benefit of the doubt she'd granted him. She shouldn't give him too much credit. Most likely he was just a crude lowlife who enjoyed making her uncomfortable with his rude remarks, even while lying at death's door. He no doubt thought her an English prig and found it a great laugh to see her squirm.

She should have left him there in the well for the Germans to find. Maybe he'd have gotten away if she hadn't hauled him up and then she wouldn't have to be bothering with him now at all.

You went all the way down into the well and you didn't even get your locket back, she chastised herself. Thinking of the locket still down in the well made her wonder anew what was in that sealed compartment. If there was ever an emergency—a valid reason to break it open and finally discover what precious thing was inside that might help her—this was it.

On the fifth day of her captivity, Emma awoke at dawn from the wide, upholstered chair that she'd been sleeping in to find the American lying on his side in the bed staring at her. For the first time, the towel that Claudine replaced three times daily when she came in to tend him and bring meals did not cover his eyes.

"Stop staring at me," she snapped. "It's rude."

"A cat can look at a queen," he replied smoothly, and again she heard his low, scratchy, Southern-inflected voice.

"What's that supposed to mean?"

"It means there's no harm in lookin', especially at someone as pretty as you."

"Well, I'm no queen, and you are certainly not a cat," she said. *No indeed,* she thought. *You're ugly as a frog! Didn't I find you at the bottom of a well? No such luck that you'd be something as lovely as a cat!*

In the last five days he'd mostly slept. While he slumbered he'd sometimes broken out in a feverish sweat and had wild, frightening dreams that caused him to cry out. He'd awoken Emma in the middle of the night screaming in a way that brought to her mind the agonized sounds she'd heard the evening of the gas attack.

"You're feeling better?" she asked, pushing a lock of disheveled hair from her face. She'd decided to try again to get on a better footing with him. They were stuck there together, after all. It would be more bearable if they could be civil to each other.

He opened his mouth to reply but before he could, the sound of a terrible explosion made him look at her with questioning, alarmed eyes.

"They've been fighting out there for five days," she told him. "The shelling has been relentless. Ground troops fire machine guns at one another all day. Hand grenades, too, I think. I don't know more than that because I haven't seen a newspaper since the Germans took over the estate."

"So I guess I'm a prisoner of war," he surmised.

"No. They don't know you were fighting with the Allies because you had no uniform on, only your long underwear. They know you're American from your accent. I told them that you lived here with me. By the way, what's your real name?"

The slightest smile appeared on his lips. "Jack Sprat."

"Oh, do come on," she chided.

"John W. Verde, from New Orleans, Louisiana, U.S. of A., but serving in Her Majesty's army."

"Don't say that too loudly," she warned, glancing anxiously at the closed door. "As I said, they don't know you're a soldier. I told them that you're my . . . my . . ."

"Your what?" he asked.

"Servant," she lied.

"Oh no, you don't. That's not going to stand. I'm nobody's servant," he objected, rising onto his elbow and this time staying elevated.

"Telling them that saved your life," she pointed out firmly. "I'm pretty sure they would have shot you, otherwise."

"I don't care! We goin' to set that straight, all right," he insisted, looking as though he intended to attempt getting out of the bed.

"Calm down," Emma urged, getting out of her chair with her blanket still wrapped around her. "I *didn't* really say you were my servant. I told them you were my husband."

"Then why'd you lie to me?"

"I don't know. The other thing . . . the husband thing . . . it was a bit awkward."

A slow grin spread across his face. Emma didn't at all appreciate the cat-who-caught-the bird quality she saw in it. It made her feel very much the trapped bird. "So we're married now, huh, sug," he said, still grinning.

She stepped closer to him so as not to be overheard but made sure to stay beyond his grasp, remembering how quickly his arm had snapped out to take hold of Claudine. "We certainly are not!" she whispered emphatically. "We are prisoners of the Germans and if they find out you're an enemy soldier, I don't know what they'll do to you. That's the only reason I said you were my husband."

"Why are they holding *you* prisoner?"

"They don't want me telling everyone that they're here. And I know how this house runs—or at least they think I do, though I really haven't the foggiest idea. Claudine and Willem do all that." She twisted her hands together anxiously. Explaining their predicament to him somehow brought the full reality of it to her.

"Don't you fret on it, princess," he said.

"Don't call me that," she objected. "I'm not a queen and neither am I a princess."

"You look like one to me," he insisted. "And this sure seems like a castle."

"It was built for one of my mother's ancestors in the sixteen hundreds but it was never a castle," she explained. He seemed determined to cast her as a haughty aristocrat and she resented it fiercely. The fact that her family had money was certainly neither a crime nor a reason she should be mocked.

"You sure this ain't a castle?" he pressed.

"Positive. And now the Germans have turned it into a military garrison. It's obvious why they wanted it. Besides the fact that it's huge, it overlooks miles and miles of fields below it."

"We'll be all right. I been in tighter spots 'an this," he said. "When I was twelve, I did time in the Waifs' Home in New Orleans."

"Waifs' Home?"

"Sort of a cross between an orphanage and a junior prison for kids on the street who broke the law. My friend Louie and I got thrown in for blowin' off firecrackers in front of a fancy hotel on New Year's Eve. I don't think our sauerkraut-eating friends here can top that experience. Man, they were tough in there. And almost as soon as I got out I was nearly picked up by the police again. Only by then I was too old for the Waifs' Home. I had to hop on out of town real fast then."

"You're a wanted criminal?" Emma cried, aghast. That would certainly explain why he was fighting with a foreign army. He was hiding from the police! Could this get any worse?

He chuckled as if it were all a joke to him. "I was over by a Storyville honky-tonk an' I'd just slipped in without payin' the admit fee to hear a guy playin' his blues guitar. I like music. In the home, my pal Louie taught me to play the cornet like he did. They were teaching him trumpet in there, but I never could play the way he did. But from Louie I got to appreciate jazz and the blues."

"Did the owners call the constables because you sneaked in?" Emma asked.

"You could say that. The owners told the police I was pickin' pockets just to have me ejected because the police wouldn't bother with sneak-ins. But then they recognized me from the Home and they decided I must have been a pickpocket, after all.

There was no way I was letting them take me to jail, so I broke loose and jumped right into the Mississippi."

The memory of his watery escape made him chuckle sleepily, which set off a fit of coughing. When it subsided, he went on. "I had to swim a fair bit before I caught up to a riverboat and climbed aboard. Those tides are powerful, all right. Good thing I swim as good as any frog; can hold my breath longer than anyone in my parish."

"Parish?"

"You might call it a county," he explained. "They held an underwater swimming contest once when I was ten years of age and I won, stayed under longer 'an fellas as old as fifteen."

The world he was describing was completely foreign to Emma. It couldn't have been any stranger if he were describing life on the moon. "How ever did you become a British soldier?" she asked.

"Little by little I made my way north to New York City, where I found some work on the docks there. New York is a rough place but thrilling in its way, and so I stood by awhile. That's why most of my Louisiana accent is changed and faded out now."

Emma smiled at that. "You have enough of it left," she assured him. "I still don't understand how you got to England."

"After a time, I got work as a deckhand on a ship going over to London. Even though the U.S. was supposed to be stayin' out of it, supply ships were coming to England almost every week. The U.S. is sending tons of food and ammunition here to the Western Front. The waters were filled with those sneaky German U-boats trying to take down the supply ships."

"U-boats? I read about them in the newspaper. What are they, exactly?"

"German submarines," he explained.

"Weren't you afraid your ship would be blown up?"

"Sure was. Our ship just barely dodged a torpedo once."

Emma sighed. "I wish the Americans would join the war. Perhaps this whole mess would be done with if we had the extra fighting power of the U.S."

"A lot of folks in the U.S. want to stay clear of it. But I say it's just a matter of time before the Germans sink one of the American ships. And that's what's goin' to get Uncle Sam into this war."

"I suppose so," she agreed. "I still don't understand how you wound up as a soldier in the British army, however."

"Simple, really. I made lots of runs back and forth across the Atlantic 'cause, even though it was dangerous, I enjoyed making the cash. We got extra for doing hazardous duty. For the first time in my life I had some money," he explained.

"In London, I got to know a lot of Brit crewmen who was enlisting every day. After a while I figured that since I might get shot at anyway, I might as well sign up to be a Tommy soldier and get the uniform."

Surely he was joking!

"You signed up to fight in order to get the uniform?" she asked incredulously.

"Yeah, you right I did," he replied. "And now I've gone and lost it. Ain't that the sorriest story you ever heard of?"

She didn't believe him. Although he was making a joke of it, a subtle sadness now underlined his jaunty tone. What didn't he want to reveal? What did this story of wanting the uniform cover? "Why weren't you wearing your uniform in the well?" she asked.

"Stripped it off," he said with a new quietness. "The poison gas was all got up in the threads and it was burning my skin like fire."

He shut his eyes again and his brow furrowed unhappily. Emma could tell that he was experiencing the terrible attack once again in memory.

"Why were you in my well?" she asked.

"Hiding from the gas. I had only one thought, to get under the water and hide from the gas. I can always find water. It's a gift I have. I can hear it singing."

"Excuse me?" she questioned. Singing water?

He closed his eyes with his head back against his pillow. His voice was fading, and he seemed to have worn himself out with talking. "Yes, indeed. Water has a song just like anything else has. If you're able to hear it, you can always find water. Because water is one of the most beautiful things on the planet, its song is one of the most beautiful."

His eyes closed.

His voice seemed to drift.

"My mam always called me her frog. Maybe it's the frog part that lets me hear the water song."

Emma watched him sleep. What an odd person he was.

She got up and, standing before the dresser mirror, did her long hair up in a bun. In the bathroom, she slipped off her long white nightgown and changed into a white blouse and an ankle-length brown skirt. She slipped her feet into stockings that she rolled at the knee and heeled ankle boots.

When she came out of the bathroom, the stone-faced German colonel was standing in the center of the room facing her.

CHAPTER EIGHT
Frog Dream

Jack wasn't really asleep, only half.

He was aware of Emma's voice in the room and a man's voice. He spoke with a German accent. He didn't like the hard tones of the German and Dutch languages. Even the Flemish, which was softer, had some of the guttural sounds. He heard it in some American dialects, too. Fortunately there was less of it in the liquid sounds of the Louisiana speech. Maybe it was the French influence. He didn't know. They kept talking as he drifted into a dream. . . .

He was on a ship, mopping the deck. The sun was extremely bright, scorching his skin. The ship rocked steadily back and forth in a way that made his stomach queasy, which surprised him. He'd never experienced seasickness before. Thinking he might lose his breakfast there on the deck, he moved to the ship's railing—better to spill it into the roiling ocean below.

He saw a line etched out on the water. For a moment he thought of alligators moving below the surface out in the bayou. *Don't take your eyes off that line for a second,* he recalled his mother telling him.

He sensed someone beside him. It was Louie, his pal from the Waifs' Home, playing the trumpet sweet as could be. "Hey, Louie. I didn't know you were on this ship," he said. "They taught you real good there in the Home."

He looked back out at the ocean. It was filled with alligators now. He could see the spiny, scaly ridges of their backs coming toward the ship. "Louie, look, there's alligators out there," he said.

But when he turned back, Louie had changed into the young soldier who'd been in the trench beside him when the gas started to spread. Instead of Louie's sweet trumpet, he was blowing a bugle as he often did at dawn and dusk. "Those are not alligators," he asserted in his working-class English accent. "Those are torpedoes."

And then everything was blinding light. Debris flew past him as a blast knocked him off his feet and sent him hurtling through the air.

He fell from the air, tumbling around and around in a circle under the water, plummeting deeper and deeper. Other bodies floated in the water all around him.

From under the water, he heard Louie's trumpet playing all around him and he suddenly turned into a frog as one of the other men on the boat floated past him. He grabbed the man's wrist in his long frog fingers and tugged him upward as he swam fast for the surface.

Louie's trumpet became louder and lost its sweet tone. It became the kid's bugle again. And then even that changed to the sound of a boat's blaring horn.

He cleared the foaming surface and pulled the man up with him. Pieces of the shattered ship were everywhere. He hoisted the unconscious man onto a floating piece of door.

The rescue boat blaring its horn came to pick up the floating man, who was another deckhand like himself. But Jack knew that since he was a frog, it was his job to go back down to see who else he could bring to the surface. So down he went, once again.

Jack awoke from his dream with his sheets in a knot around his legs. He wondered if he'd been kicking as he swam in his dream; that famous super frog kick of his that won him every swimming contest. Funny that he'd dreamed of becoming a frog. Probably because he'd just been telling Emma how his mother called him her frog. His big sister Louisa had said that his raspy voice was a frog voice; she was so good to him otherwise that he didn't hold it against her.

So many memories had mixed together in his dream. It was odd, he thought, that he should dream about the U-boat attack on his ship when he'd gone out of his way not to mention it to Emma. It hadn't even been reported to the American public because the politicians in Washington were committed to keeping America out of this Great War.

He hadn't told her about the explosion because he didn't want to think about it, much less talk about it. It had been the real reason, though, that he'd signed up.

He saw what a mess the British were in, what they were really up against. He had lived it now first-hand. Later, when he spent the time recovering in the British hospital, he heard more stories from the Western Front, awful, heartbreaking stories.

He couldn't sit by and do nothing to help. The day they released him from the hospital, he'd walked out and gone directly to sign up.

He laughed lightly to himself, wondering if she really believed he'd signed up to get the dowdy khaki uniform with its putty-colored heavy leggings and metal pie-pan helmet.

What a pretty girl she was, and so brave to climb down there and get him from the well. She had a prickly side, he could tell, but it only made him smile. He liked her fire. She was smart, too, reading the papers and all the way she did; speaking German and French so well. He admired intelligent people, often wished he'd spent more time in school.

He got up on his elbow and looked around. Where had she gone?

That colonel had better not be bothering her. He might be too weak to help her now but he intended to be better very soon.

CHAPTER NINE
Mata Hari

The colonel, who told her his name was Colonel Hans Schiller, asked Emma to walk with him around the grounds of the estate. When she'd first encountered him she'd been in such a state of panic, intent on matching his arrogance so as not to seem intimidated. She'd been so focused on saying just the right things that she'd barely been able to take in his appearance at all.

But now she saw that he was much younger than she'd originally thought, somewhere in his twenties. Tall, blond, and with pale blue eyes, he would have been good-looking if she'd been able to forget he was the enemy.

She'd accompanied him out of her bedroom and down the hall to the main stairs leading into the grand foyer of the estate, amazed at the transformation in her home. The once echoing, empty building now bustled with German soldiers moving briskly in every direction. Cabbagy smells of meals filled the hallways. Descending the stairway, she saw that the ornate furniture of the elegant main living room had been pushed up against the walls to make space for the rows of soldiers' cots.

At the front entrance, Old Willem was mending a broken panel on the door and nodded to her unhappily as she went by. Emma assumed that he and Claudine had been pressed into service by the Germans.

Once outside, she and the colonel walked side by side without talking. Though overcast, the wet warmth of April hung in the air and a balmy breeze ruffled the loose fringes of her hair. Today there were no sounds of fighting or approaching planes. Emma's spirits lifted with the sheer relief of being outdoors after having been confined in her room for so long.

Not far from the well, Colonel Schiller stopped to gaze out over the fields. "The quiet is good, yes?" he commented in German.

"Very good," she agreed, also speaking in German.

He became lost in thought for a moment before he spoke again. "We should enjoy the quiet while it lasts. Your countrymen along with their French, Canadian, and Belgian allies will surely attempt to take this position from us at some point. It is too good a vantage point from which to see the advancing soldiers in the fields below. They cannot afford to let us keep it. They will try to fight us for this ridge."

His words frightened her. She'd seen what had

happened to Ypres. If a village could be destroyed, so could the estate. "How close will they get?" she asked.

He grinned disdainfully. "Not close at all, if we are successful at defeating them down in the fields. I do not think you need to worry."

Emma felt keenly the uncomfortable divide this situation was causing in her loyalties. She should want the Allies to come very close and take The Ridge. If they controlled the area, she might even make it safely to the port at the French city of Calais, where she could get a boat across the English Channel and finally go home.

Yet she didn't want any harm to come to the estate, or to be in the middle of horrific missile fire and shooting as she had that day in Ypres. She never wanted to experience anything like that again.

"Tell me . . . really . . . why you were in that well," Colonel Schiller said, glancing into the well.

Emma looked up at him sharply. "I told you what happened."

"Why did he not simply go inside your lovely home?"

"He was out of his mind with pain and wasn't thinking clearly. Besides, he thought the water would soothe the burning." She was glad he'd been able to give her at least that much information.

"You do not seem to be on very close terms with your husband," he observed. "I see that the servant woman tends him. Should not a wife take care of her husband?"

"Claudine is more experienced at such things than I am," she replied. "I want Jack to have the best care, and she can give it."

"You are both quite young. When were you married?"

"Last year, in New Orleans," Emma said. "He's the son of a business associate of my father."

"The date?"

"July 6, 1914," she said, naming the date of her last birthday so she'd be sure to remember what she'd said. "Jack is a jazz musician. He plays the coronet."

"What is jazz?"

"It's a type of music, very big in America."

"You like this jazz?" he asked.

"Truthfully, I'm more of a ragtime girl, but jazz is the newest thing."

Colonel Schiller smiled a moment, and then his face grew serious. "Mrs. Sprat, since you speak both German and English, I have a proposal to make to you," he said. "Once a week I will allow you to accompany your servant couple to the market to buy fresh food and anything else you require. In return, you will keep a sharp ear open for any talk you may hear of an Allied attack upon The Ridge."

"You want me to spy?" she asked in surprise.

With a slight smile, he nodded. "Why not? It could prove quite exciting for you, and lucrative; not that such a thing would matter to a young woman of your class. But then again, times are changing. Spoils of war go to the victor, which will be Germany and

Austria. The defeated will suffer many reversals of fortune. If you show talent at it, we could even send you to our spy academy in Antwerp. It's run by a woman, you know, Elsbeth Schragmuller, a stern taskmaster but a brilliant spy. Have you heard of Margaretha Zelle?"

Emma recalled the name. She'd read about her in a magazine the girls were passing around in school. "Mata Hari?" she asked, recalling the dancer's stage name.

"Yes. She is spying for us and doing quite well."

Now there's a piece of information! she thought. She'd be sure to tell the Allies if she ever got the chance.

"Perhaps you do not care for the payment," the colonel went on. "If you bring me back useful information, I will instead consider allowing you and your husband to leave on a ship bound for America."

"You'd let us go?" Emma blurted excitedly.

He nodded. "But only if you bring me back facts that are vital to defeating the Allies."

He wanted her to be a spy—a traitor to her own country! "If caught, I could be shot for such an offense!" she reminded him.

"Or *we* could simply shoot you right now," he pointed out coolly. "But if you are useful to us, we would be less inclined to do so."

She opened her mouth to speak, but no words came out.

"It is something I would deeply regret having to do," he added. "I hope you do not force my hand."

℧   ℧   ℧

At dusk, Emma was once again curled up in her chair while Jack slept. She'd told Colonel Schiller that if she heard anything, she'd report it to him. It seemed like the safest thing to say when threatened with being shot.

She had no intention of doing it, of course. To betray one's own country—what could be lower?

She tapped the arm of the chair thoughtfully. Might there be a way to turn the situation to her advantage; to appear to be providing information without actually doing so? She had to think about it more.

If only there was some way to get out of here and over to the port at Dunkirk, she could tell the Allies everything she knew about the Germans: how many troops they had, how much ammunition she'd seen stacked in bags around the walls of the estate, how many trucks were parked by the front entrance. She could reveal to them that there was a spy school in Antwerp and that the dancer known as Mata Hari was spying for the Germans.

The idea both thrilled and frightened her. Could she ever really have the nerve for such a thing? Sneaking out of the Hampshire School to meet Lloyd at night was the most daring thing she'd ever done before. And though the punishment would have been severe if she had been caught, no one would have shot her. Her big adventure with Lloyd now seemed laughably safe and inconsequential compared to her current predicament.

Maybe she could bribe a soldier into letting her escape. But what did she have to offer? Colonel Schiller had confiscated her purse; apparently the idea had occurred to him, as well. He'd also taken her mother's jewelry box, demanded the code to the safe, and even removed her mother's furs.

This was no doubt just the sort of emergency that her great-grandmother had been referring to when she'd said there was something in the locket to help her. If only she could get it back.

Jack stirred in his sleep, mumbling what sounded like a warning to someone. He cried out, his agitation growing.

Emma went to him as he began to thrash in the bed. "Wake up! You're dreaming. Wake up!"

His eyes opened, filled with panic. "I was in the well. It was fillin' up with gas. I tried to climb out, but somebody sealed the top," he told her, still agitated. "I was pushin' an' pushin' but the lid wouldn't budge."

"It was just a dream," she assured him.

He blinked at her hard, slowly coming fully awake. "You okay, sug?" he asked.

"Fine."

"That colonel didn't bother you?"

"No."

"You tell me if he does, you hear?"

As if he could do anything about it if she was in danger. He was so weak and injured, he could barely sit up in bed for long.

"He told me that the dancer they call Mata Hari is

56

a German spy," she said as his eyes began to close again.

"He told you that?" he murmured.

"Yes."

"Maybe he just wants you to think so," he said, his eyes closed, his voice drifting.

"Why would he want that?"

"In case you might tell someone," he said. "Maybe she's an Allied spy and he wants the Allies to distrust her information."

"I never thought of that," she admitted.

"In this war, you always have to be thinking." He turned his head and began to snore lightly.

He's right, she thought. Although he had little formal education, in so many ways he was smarter than she was. Maybe not smarter, really, but more aware of how the real world worked. He looked at things in ways she might not even consider because he had experienced life. Every time she talked to him she felt as if she learned something new, saw things from a different angle. She respected that.

As she stood beside him, she recalled his story of winning the underwater swimming contest. Perhaps if he ever did get better, she might persuade him to go down into the well to search for the locket for her. Though his injuries were extensive, he did appear to be improving quite fast. And swimming underwater apparently came naturally to him. It wouldn't be such a difficult thing to ask of him.

Suddenly, she could hardly wait for him to get better.

☙ ☙ ☙

Several days later, on Saturday, Colonel Schiller sent for Emma shortly after breakfast. In his hand he held the small, blue beaded purse he had confiscated and handed it to her. "You will go with your servants to the market. While they shop for food, you will buy whatever you might require. Do not hesitate to linger . . . and to listen."

Tucking the purse into the cuff of her long-sleeved blouse, she nodded. "I understand," she said.

Putting on a lightweight dusty blue jacket and her matching hat with the band of violets just above the brim, she met Willem and Claudine in the front. Willem had brought around the horse-drawn wagon he liked to use on the estate. The huge Belgian draft horse with its chestnut coat and white blaze in the center of its broad head struck her as a creature that had walked out of another time period—one so much saner—and she was cheered by the sight of it. Claudine gestured for her to sit beside Willem in front, but Emma declined, happy to sit alone on bushels of hay in the wagon in back.

Spring was once again in the air as she held her face up to the warming sun. She could hardly believe she was being allowed to go to the market. It made her long to be home and free again more intensely than ever. She could even stand putting in her last few months at the Hampshire School in order to graduate.

Her mind began to race with possibilities. How hard could it be to slip away in the crowd at the market? She wouldn't want Claudine and Willem to be blamed. Perhaps they might want to escape too. She wished she could speak to them.

Her thoughts of escape were cut short when a German soldier, barrel-chested and expressionless, climbed into the back with her. He sat in the far corner of the wagon, his bayonet-tipped rifle slung over his shoulder, and didn't make eye contact even for a second. Another soldier, similarly remote and intimidating, soon joined them.

As the wagon moved forward, Emma pulled the purse from her sleeve. Did it contain enough to bribe them to let her escape? She counted out the money. It wasn't a huge sum—but it was worth a try.

The wagon hit a rut in the road, and she used the opportunity to thrust the money out onto the hay. Both soldiers looked down at it immediately. "It's yours if you allow me to wander away while we are in the market," she told them in German.

A joyless smile came to the first soldier's lips. "Do you think that is worth the price we would pay for letting you escape?" he snarled. "Pick it up and do not insult us further."

Flushing with humiliation, Emma gathered up her money and sat back in the corner. She needed something more valuable to barter for her freedom— she absolutely had to get that locket back.

CHAPTER TEN
Claudine's Plan

Jack awoke and looked up at Claudine, who was mopping his sweaty brow. "You were dreaming again," she said in French that was heavily accented with her native Flemish. "What terrible dreams they must be to make you sweat so."

"You speak French?" he questioned, speaking with his own Louisiana version of the language that so many spoke in the French city of New Orleans. Although he wasn't fluent like Emma, he spoke enough to understand and make himself understood.

"I am learning more every day," Claudine confided. "I want to help our cause, and to do that I must speak French or English but the English is too difficult. I need your help because you speak both French and English."

"Emma speaks both," he pointed out.

Claudine shook her head. "I don't want to endanger

her. She's so young. Do not tell of this. It is best that she does not know. I have to tell you quickly before she comes in. Right now she is down in the stable helping Willem groom the horse. She has a fondness for horses."

"What can I do?"

"They are bringing more supplies and ammunition here every day. They are preparing for something. When I go to market, Willem and I know people there who can pass that information on to the Allied armies across enemy lines. We need the information to be put in a code and in English. You are a soldier. Do you know what kind of codes the British would understand?"

"I was delivering a coded message when I got caught in the gas attack," he told her. "I know how the code worked."

"Very good. Then I can count on you?"

"A hundred percent."

CHAPTER ELEVEN
A Promise

One week later, Emma awoke to find Jack sitting up with his legs slung over the side of the four-poster bed. For the first time he looked strong enough to actually get out of bed and it appeared as though that was what he intended to attempt next. She wondered if he'd be strong enough.

Standing, he crossed to the mirror above the dresser and inspected his image for the first time since he'd arrived, smoothing his wild black curls. His peeled skin was healing and the blisters on his lips, though papery and raw, were improving. The swelling of his eye area was almost, though not quite, gone.

Emma decided he looked like a complete wild man. But, though she would never admit it, she found something attractive in the wildness—a thing raw and vibrant with energy. Considering that he had been half dead when she first encountered him, he now seemed more alive than anyone she'd ever known.

Judging from the grin spreading across his face, he was pleased with what he saw. Turning to her, he pointed at his image in the mirror. "Who is that handsome devil?" he asked playfully. "I'd say he looks good enough to kiss. Want to try?"

"Would you please stop it?" she exploded, all the more distressed by the request because he seemed to have realized she had been privately assessing his attractiveness. It unnerved her, this ability of his to intuit her thoughts. She refused to believe he could actually read her mind no matter how much it seemed to be the case. Nonetheless this power of his was uncanny and she didn't like feeling he had any power over her. "Stop asking me for a kiss," she insisted. "If you haven't figured it out by now, let me tell you again—it is never going to happen!"

"Ah, I guess you're too fancy to kiss a guy like me," he said lightly, "even though it would be so nice."

He was too impossible! He delighted in underlining the fact that he was uneducated and without refinement of any sort. When she mentioned even the most commonplace nicety, such as the fact that she missed having afternoon tea, he laughed his low, chortling chuckle, joking, "Ah, well, I wouldn't know about any of that, sug. I'll have to go ask the queen."

When he mocked her that way, it made her want to strangle him. It was as if he saw her as some upper-class twit, an image of herself that she did not want to hold, even for a moment.

"I bet you don't even know the queen's name," she'd challenged him one afternoon.

"Queen Mary of Teck, wife of George the Fifth," he answered correctly. "You sure do think I'm dumb, don't you?"

"I think you only say the things you do in order to make me angry because, to you, it's some sort of amusement."

"That's not so," he disagreed. "I ask for a kiss because I want you to kiss me and show you like me a little."

"You *don't* want a kiss at all," she insisted. "You only say it because you think it's funny to upset me."

"Your eyes do go wide with shock and alarm," he admitted.

"See! I knew it!"

"But they're such pretty eyes."

Even now she couldn't tell if he meant it or if he was only making fun of her. "Why does it delight you so much to tease me?" she demanded.

"Ah, come on, sug, don't be that way," he said now, settling back on the bed. "I'm only playin'. We're stuck here together like this. I just want to be friends with you."

"Then you don't really want me to kiss you?"

"Yeah, I want a kiss!" he insisted emphatically. "But it could be a nice friendly kiss. It don't have to be a kiss you'd read about in a romance novel."

"I wouldn't know. I've never read one."

"But you get the gist of my meaning," he insisted.

She realized from the new energy that had come into his movements and his voice that he really was much stronger than he had been. He was probably even finally strong enough to go down into the well to search under the water for her locket.

"I don't want to fight with you," she began in a new, conciliatory tone of voice. "You're right. Under the circumstances, we should try to be friends. I enjoyed hearing about your boyhood. It's so interesting that you're able to hold your breath for so long. How did you come by that ability?"

"I've always loved to swim," he said. "My mam taught me when I was a baby, before I could even walk."

"I thought you were in a home for orphans."

"Not always. My daddy was never around, but my mam took good care of me before she passed on when I was ten. She taught me a lot."

"Like how to hold your breath under water?"

That made him chuckle. "Naw. That just came to me natural. An old fisherman taught me how to pump the air up from the bottom of my lungs when . . . ah, never mind. You don't want to hear it."

"I do," she insisted. She was interested in anything that had to do with his ability to stay under water.

"Why do you want to know about my breath-holding ability?" he asked, as if reading her mind yet again.

"The day I found you in the well, I was searching

for a locket I had thrown down there. I would very much like it back and I was wondering if—when you're strong enough, of course—you could manage to retrieve it for me."

He studied her skeptically. "What's so special about it?" he asked. "Got a picture of your boyfriend in there?"

"My parents."

"Then why'd you throw it in the well?"

"I forgot the picture was in there at the moment I threw it. I was angry about something else. I regretted it the instant I remembered that their picture was in the locket," she replied.

He nodded, studying her. "Why should I get it for you?"

"I thought you wanted to be friends."

"If you're my friend, then give me the friendly kiss I asked for," he countered.

"If you're *my* friend, you'll get the locket for me," she said.

"Uh-uh," he said, shaking his head. "You first."

They stood for a moment looking at each other stubbornly, locked in a silent battle of wills.

"Then we are obviously not meant to be friends," she said, breaking the deadlock.

He turned away from her and spoke without facing her. "If I were to get this locket for you," he went on, his voice quiet and with intensity she had never heard there before, "would you then become my friend?"

"Of course," she agreed eagerly.

"Don't answer me so quick, sug," he said, his voice still low and earnest. "Make sure you understand what I'm really asking. Would you become my dearest, most loyal soul companion?"

This new seriousness in him frightened her. Why was this so important to him? "I could promise you that I would sincerely try," she replied, "to be friends, that is. I can't promise anything more than friendship."

"True friendship," he pressed. "You're sure?"

"Yes! I promise!"

A distant boom made her jump. "Another attack!" she gasped.

"Calm yourself, sug," he said. "It's only thunder."

It rained all that night but on the next day, while Jack napped, Colonel Schiller opened the bedroom door and beckoned for Emma to join him in the hallway. "You heard nothing in the marketplace the other day?" he inquired, getting directly to his point.

She hadn't, but it might help her situation to have something to tell him. "I overheard some farmers saying that the Americans are secretly sending supplies to England." Even though she was sure he already knew this, she wanted to seem compliant.

"Ach!" he scoffed. "That is not news. Tomorrow our submarine U-20 will torpedo an American cruise liner that is smuggling in arms. We know all about that!"

The news hit Emma like a punch in the stomach.

There would be innocent passengers on a cruise liner.

"Arrogant Americans," he said. "Our embassy even warned them that we're onto their tricks and we intend to torpedo the liner. Only one passenger out of over a thousand canceled his ticket. Is your husband like his countrymen, so full of foolish pride?"

"My husband is not like most Americas," she said, thinking that Jack was not like *anybody* she'd ever met.

"I suppose you think he's special just because he is your husband."

"Perhaps," she agreed just to be polite. "I'm sorry the news isn't valuable to you. I am not really up on world events or political issues."

He looked her over and nodded. "That is not surprising in one so lovely as you. In the future, tell me all that you hear and I will decide what is important. You've done well enough for your first trip out."

"I'm glad," she said as sweetly as she could manage. "Do you think I might take a walk just around the outside of the estate? It's such a beautiful day, and I would love some air."

"There are guards all around the property. It will do you no good to attempt to escape."

"I won't. Thank you." She hurried down the hallway, grabbed her light coat from the closet, and went out. It was even warmer than the day before, perfect weather for what she intended to do.

Jack had intimated that he might go down the well to get the locket for her but he hadn't mentioned it in the last three days. She'd asked him again just that morning but he'd pretended he hadn't heard before turning his head and feigning sleep. "Will you go or won't you?" she'd demanded, shaking his shoulder.

"The time isn't right," he'd replied before shutting his eyes again.

If he wouldn't go down the well to search for her locket, who needed him? She'd do it herself.

CHAPTER TWELVE
A Desperate Search

Why did that girl want the locket so badly? Jack was in no hurry to get it for her. She wanted the picture of her parents? He was doubtful. Most likely it contained a picture of some boyfriend back in London, some good-for-nothing, aristocratic fop with soft, manicured hands who never did a day's work and who had an oh-so-proper British accent, and who would only break her heart in the end.

It would be better for her if that locket stayed at the bottom of the well.

He was rummaging through the drawers of all the dressers in the room, taking advantage of the fact that Emma had secured Colonel Schiller's permission to go for a walk. *I'm keeping an eye on that guy*, he thought protectively as he dug through her father's lavish assortment of silk ties and handkerchiefs. *He's a little too fond of her, if you ask me. He's trying to make her like him.*

He pulled open another drawer and went through the socks. Her father had socks as soft as baby's hair. What a different life these people led.

His thoughts drifted back to the locket as he pulled open one drawer after the other. He'd seen it falling down like some misguided shooting star back when he was in the well, right after the gas attack. How could he miss it? It had hit him, setting off a violent attack of coughing. It was down there somewhere, and he had no doubt that he could find it.

He quickly glanced at the bedroom door to check that she wasn't coming in. If she caught him at this, she would assume he was stealing. It would be a natural-enough assumption, he supposed, considering he'd revealed his spotted history with the police. When he saw the look of alarm on her face, he'd instantly wished he could call back his words. But, the damage was done. He was not only ignorant in her eyes, but criminal as well. Considering that he hadn't done anything really wrong, it seemed very unfair, but then, when had anything ever been fair?

That she thought him dangerous irked him less than that she assumed he was stupid, as if being born without privilege or much access to education made a person feebleminded. He knew, though, that his wounded air of superiority wasn't entirely justified. He hadn't been entirely honest with her, either.

It wasn't her friendship he wanted.

He didn't care for some bland, sisterly kiss. But he would settle for it because friendship would be a good place to start. It would be a beginning, anyway.

He closed the last drawer, slamming it in frustration. "Don't these people read?" he muttered. Claudine had brought him a count of the soldiers garrisoned at the estate as well as how many days' worth of food rations they had stockpiled. To put it into coded form, he needed a book. It could be any book, but it had to be one whose title the Allies would recognize and would be able to find.

Thinking about how to get his hands on a book, he wandered over to the window, gazing absently down at the pond and the well. His eyes traveled across the miles and miles of rolling fields that were visible from there. The Germans had gained a real prize when they took over this estate. The vantage point it gave them was invaluable.

He could see the dark, zigzag lines of the trenches in the distance. Were the French still down there or had the gas attack routed them for good? Were the British and Canadians ever able to join them as they had been planning? It frustrated him not to know.

A movement by the well caught his eye.

It was Emma, lingering near the well, turning her lovely face to the sun as if luxuriating in its rays. She appeared perfectly relaxed and casual. Too casual. She was up to something—and it worried him.

He had to find a way to get to her. She might need his help.

There were guards at the door, but that was all right. He'd discovered another way out, discovered it quite by accident one day. When he'd first felt well enough to get out of bed, he'd gone into the bathroom to wash himself. A sudden spell of faintness had sent him careening into the closet, groping at anything to keep from falling to the floor, leading to his discovery of a secret passage.

But getting out that way wasn't easily done, and he hoped he'd make it down to her in time, should she need him. Hurrying to the bathroom, he pulled open the linen closet door and began removing the shelves.

CHAPTER THIRTEEN
Drowning

Emma leaned against the well, turning her face up to the sun. From time to time she swung around, settling her elbows nonchalantly on the well's rim. The casualness of her movement disguised the acuity with which she was taking in her surroundings as she moved.

There was a soldier standing on the rock wall closest to the woods guarding the perimeter of the estate. Another guarded the back entrance to the estate over by the garden shed, and a third was stationed on the far side of the pond.

She checked into the well, happy to discover that the ladder had not been removed. Half the water below was illuminated by reflected sunlight. In the dark half, she saw something glisten.

Could it be her locket?

Turning back toward the estate she noticed someone in the bedroom window looking down. She could tell from his dark hair that it was Jack. In the next moment, he moved back inside the room and she no longer saw him.

It didn't matter if he knew she was getting the locket herself. It would be good, even. He'd see that she was capable of fending for herself, that she wasn't some *princess*, as he was so keen on implying, a defenseless, simpering girl who relied on his help. Why she cared what he thought was a mystery; though for some odd reason, she did seem to care.

Bending slowly, she unbuttoned her boots and peeled down her stockings. Lifting each foot out, she stretched lazily.

In the next minute, a soldier came to relieve the guard by the pond. She saw that the soldier by the back entrance was distracted by their movement. A quick check told her that the soldier on the wall was gazing dreamily out into the woods.

Moving quickly, she hoisted herself onto the well's stone rim. Swiftly swinging her legs over and onto the ladder, she tucked her head down below the edge of the well. It had taken less than a minute.

She listened. There was no shout of alarm or call to halt. Satisfied that they hadn't seen her, she began to descend.

As she came closer to the water, the golden item in the water became easier to see. She became nearly certain it was her locket.

"Oh!" She gasped as her foot touched water much sooner than it had during her previous visit to the well.

"All that rain," she murmured. It had collected in the well and raised the water level considerably. To retrieve the locket, she would have to dive completely under.

Looking up, she considered going back.

Her locket was so close, though. Its chain seemed to be stuck on a crack in the stone. If she could only grab it, it might change everything. She could bribe the guards to let her escape.

Without further thought, she drew in a large breath and plunged into the chill water, swimming downward as best she could despite the narrowness of her skirt and the billowing sleeves of her blouse. Reaching the locket, she tugged on it, but it wouldn't come loose. After a few minutes of working its chain from the stone with hurried fingers, she had to abandon the task and return to the surface, hungrily sucking in air as she came above the water.

Once more, inhaling deeply, she went back under to get the locket, swimming down to the spot where she thought she'd last been.

The locket wasn't there.

Had it come loose and sunk even lower into the well?

Peering down, she flailed her arms in place to keep from floating up. She saw no sign of the locket but she had to go deeper to be sure it wasn't there.

Clasping the stones, she moved down, her eyes darting to every corner as she worked her way lower and lower. Several air bubbles escaped her lips. Too soon she would have to resurface for air.

A moment later, the straining sensation in her lungs warned that time was up. She lifted her head in order to rise but she did not ascend more than several inches. Instead, her ankle throbbed with sudden pain.

It was stuck in a crack in the wall.

A second pull only caused the pain to intensify.

Bending, she tried to wiggle it free. *Come on*, she thought anxiously as more air bubbles floated from her lips.

She hadn't even realized that she'd been resting her foot in the broken opening. When she'd tried to rise she'd somehow lifted it into this narrower space. But how had she turned her ankle to manage it? She couldn't reproduce the same motion to extricate her wedged foot and ankle.

Her straining lungs were now aching for air. She fought down the panicky urge to call out for help, knowing it was terror clouding her judgment.

Her head swirled dizzily as undulating black blobs pulsated before her eyes. She'd fainted in church one summer and recognized the warning signs that she was losing consciousness now.

Her imagination sent her a grisly image of herself floating there, still tethered by her ankle to the wall, hair wafting above her head, her skin bloated and translucently white, purple lips agape.

She was only dimly aware of a large, dark form moving toward her, seeming to rise from the water below. It stopped just below her, and she felt a strong grip surround her ankle.

CHAPTER FOURTEEN
Opening the Locket

Jack laid Emma on the bed, relieved to see the rhythmic rise and fall of her breath. With her dark hair in a wet tangle around her head, he thought she had never looked more beautiful.

Unexpectedly, her eyes snapped open, filled with wild panic. "How did I get here?" she demanded.

"I looked out the window and saw you lying there on the grass next to the well, passed out," he said. "I called the soldiers and they carried you up here."

There was no sense telling her the truth. If he explained how he'd gotten down there into the well, he'd have to tell her too much.

Her hand went to her mouth and she trembled as tears filled her eyes. He put his hand on her shoulder comfortingly. "It's okay, sug. You're okay now."

She sat up, shrugging her shoulder out from

under his hand. "There's something in that well. It saved me from drowning."

"I told you I'd get the fool locket for you. Why'd you go down there, anyway?" he asked, changing the subject.

"You were taking too long," she replied.

He sat on the edge of the bed and studied her. Why had she gotten to him like this?

He thought about her all the time.

When she wasn't there he worried about her safety. He played and replayed every conversation they had in his mind, turning over everything she said in search of hidden meaning as though the words themselves were smooth, shining river stones he'd saved to reflect on in private.

She was willful and headstrong, impetuous and bossy; also brave and independent. And there were flashes of tenderness just below her surface, though it took a sharp eye and ear to catch them; sometimes it was no more than a softness creeping into her voice that gave her away.

He had begun to love her for all those reasons, both the good and the more dubious qualities he saw in her. Besides, he knew she had saved his life, although now, he supposed, they were even.

"What's that in your hand?" she asked sharply.

He curled his fingers more tightly around the golden sphere of the locket, but it was too late to hide the bit of chain that showed. She lunged for his fist, wrapping it in her own two hands as she tried to pry his fingers loose. "Give it to me," she insisted. "It's mine!"

He easily pulled his hand away as he got off the bed. "Not so fast. You promised to be my true friend if I got it for you. Do you intend to honor that promise?"

"But you didn't get it for me. You never went down in the well."

"Maybe I did and maybe I didn't," he said, toying with her. "The fact is that I have your locket and if I give it to you, I will have fulfilled my part of the bargain."

"You didn't go down to get it," she insisted.

"Maybe I've had it since the first day that it clonked me on the head." That wasn't how it had happened. He'd only just found it wedged, like her foot had been, between two jagged stones under the water, but it was possible he'd had it all along, and so that would be his story.

"And you didn't return it to me?" she cried. "You're horrible!"

"That's sort of harsh, sug," he replied, still holding tight to the locket. "I may be a little rough around the edges but I'm not horrible. I was just waitin' for the right moment."

Again, she lunged for his fist. He quickly switched it behind his back to the other hand and held it out to her in the center of his flat palm. "Here you go."

In a flash of movement, she plucked it from his hand and moved swiftly away over to the upholstered chair, eyeing him warily. He lay on the bed and put his hands behind his head. "Don't worry. I'm not going to try to get it back. I gave it to you of my own will, didn't I?"

He watched her open the locket and gaze down at the photo inside. His vision remained somewhat foggy from the gas but he suspected that the photo under the glass was ruined. "Boyfriend's handsome face wrecked?" he asked.

Ignoring his comment, she attempted to get her fingernail under the golden frame and pick it up, but couldn't move it.

He went to the dresser where he found a pen. "Let me try," he offered, his hand outstretched to take the locket from her.

She shot him a suspicious glance.

"I'll return it to you," he assured her with a note of annoyance behind his words. Why would he have given it to her if he intended to snatch it away again?

Examining the locket, he saw the blurred picture. Whatever the boyfriend had looked like, he would never know. That was all right. He didn't particularly want to see him. She sure was frantic to get at that picture, though. It wounded him to see how badly she wanted it.

He stuck the pen nib into the frame and gently lifted the frame and glass before handing it to her.

Without a glance, she peeled off the top picture. Quickly crumpling it and tossing it to the floor, she gently smoothed with her thumb the photograph that lay below it.

He came beside her and looked down at the picture in the open locket. The edges of the picture were somewhat damaged by the water, but the people were still visible. They were a very proper-looking man and woman. The woman, though, had lively eyes and Jack saw where Emma had gotten her striking beauty and defiant expression.

For a moment, Emma sat there, transfixed by the faces in the locket, her eyes brimming with tears. So it hadn't been the boyfriend she was after at all, he realized. He could see how much this meant and felt guilty for doubting her and for teasing her about it.

After a moment, she brusquely brushed her eyes dry and looked up at him. "Do you think you could open the other side of the locket for me?" she requested.

He reached out and she placed the locket in his palm. Prying again with the pen nib into the compartment on the other half of the sphere, he attempted to open it, but this time nothing budged. He lifted it to his ear and shook it. "What's in there?"

"I don't know. I've never been able to open it." She looked up at him seriously. "Did you see anyone else around the well?" she asked. "Someone saved me. Whoever it was swam up at me from the bottom of the well."

"Maybe it was some kind of water creature, half man, half frog," he suggested. He didn't want to reveal how he'd gotten into the well. She might try it herself, and it was incredibly dangerous.

"Don't be absurd," she scoffed. "But, still . . . it's

quite odd." She lifted her hand. "My locket, please."

He didn't give it back to her immediately. "Now can I collect my friendly kiss?"

She got up from the chair and cast him an offended glance. "If you don't mind, I've just been nearly drowned. I'd like to find a towel to dry my hair, and to put on some dry clothing."

He stood there feeling her rebuff like a slap. Granted, until now he'd been making this request lightly, as if it were a joke, but that had been to cover his insecurity. He'd never really believed then that she would kiss him.

This time, though, he had dared to think that something had changed. . . .

Apparently not.

Finding dry clothing in her drawer, she headed for the small bathroom. She closed the door with a slight bang and latched the lock decisively. Something in the resolute clack of the lock told him she had locked him out in every way possible and that she had no intention of ever being his friend or anything more.

"But we made a deal," he said quietly.

CHAPTER FIFTEEN
Something New

"Hey, sug, anything to read around here?" Jack asked the next morning. "I mean, is there a book in this place?"

Emma was brushing her hair in front of the mirror and turned slowly toward him. "There's a library downstairs."

"What?" he questioned.

"You heard me."

"I hear you, but I don't get it," he replied. "How can the library be in a person's home? Do people around here come in and borrow books from you?"

She rolled her eyes impatiently. "It's not the *public* library. It's my parents' library."

"That sure beats all," he said, clearly surprised. "I've never heard of such a thing. Imagine having your own library. And there it was right underneath me all the time."

She suppressed a smile, pleased to have impressed him with something *she* knew, for a change. He must be truly amazed—too stunned to make fun of her or say he'd have to ask the queen about it or some other jab. Maybe he was trying to be more civil, to be more of a friend.

She would try too. Truly she felt just a bit guilty for not giving him his friendly kiss. She owed him after he'd given her the locket and even opened it for her. She just couldn't believe he would be so crude as to want the kiss right after she'd nearly drowned! It had annoyed her and she'd reacted without thinking. Today she would try to make it up to him.

She twisted her hair up and pinned it. "Do you want something from the library?"

"Name me an English book everyone would know," he requested.

"Maybe something by Charles Dickens? *Oliver Twist? Great Expectations?*" she suggested.

"*Great Expectations!*" he decided immediately. "I like the sound of that! Come to think of it, bring me both those books."

"All right. When Colonel Schiller comes by, I'll ask if we can go to the library." She wondered if he would really read the books or if he was simply trying to impress her, to show that he was as literate as she.

"An' yes I *can* read!" he added, once again seeming to read her mind. "I might be a little slower than you are in reading, but I did go to school—at least while my mam was alive."

85

Caught again! How did he do it? Were her thoughts really that transparent?

"I didn't say you couldn't," she replied, trying to sound casual, but turning so he couldn't see the blush rising in her cheeks. She suddenly felt embarrassed by her snobbery, for feeling superior about the imbalance in their reading skills.

That afternoon, Emma prevailed on Colonel Schiller to allow them to visit the library on the second floor. He told her that she could go, but not Jack. "He should rest," he said.

"I bet he wants to escort you there by himself," Jack grumbled when she told him the news. "I think he's sweet for you. Be careful of him."

She shushed him, knowing that Colonel Schiller was waiting just outside the door to escort her down to the library. "That's ridiculous," she scoffed, even though the same thought had lately occurred to her.

Emma got the two Dickens books for Jack and picked out *Pride and Prejudice* by Jane Austen for herself. When she returned to the room, she found him sitting on a straight chair by the window, gazing out at ominous thunder clouds rolling in from over the fields. Crossing to him, she handed him the thick, heavy volumes.

"Are your eyes strong enough to read?" she asked. The swelling was almost all gone, and she noticed that he actually had very nice eyes, deep brown rimmed with thick black lashes, but they seemed unfocused sometimes and she wondered how much of his vision had returned.

"Sometimes it's better than other times," he answered vaguely, taking the books from her. "Thank you for getting me the books."

"You're welcome." She had the satisfying feeling of having done something friendly for him. It made her feel she'd done her best to keep up her end of the promise. In the future she would try to find other friendly gestures she could make that wouldn't involve kissing.

"What book have you got there?" he asked. She held up the cover so he could read it. "*Pride and Prejudice*, huh? Hey, that's me and you."

"I don't understand," she said, suddenly on guard against another taunt.

"I think you do," he replied with a smirk, opening *Oliver Twist* as though the subject were closed.

How could she be friends with him when he criticized her at every opportunity? Oh, he was too exasperating! He was not going to just get away with it this time!

"No! I have absolutely no idea what you mean by that," she insisted as she settled into the upholstered chair with the book.

"Yeah, you do," he insisted.

"Well, maybe I do," she shouted, getting up again angrily, "if what you mean is that you are annoyingly proud and prejudiced against *me* because my parents have money. Because all I can see is that you are constantly jabbing at me, implying that I am a silly rich girl and that you are somehow better than me, more *real*, because you don't have money!"

"That's funny!" he shot back, also standing, equally angry. "All *I* see is you looking down your nose at me and acting like I'm a low-class fool that you have to put up with 'cause we're stuck together in this room!"

His outburst took her by surprise, mostly because she didn't think of him that way at all. At first, possibly, there had been some of that in her opinion of him. But it wasn't what she thought now.

He was clever, intuitive, and resourceful. And good company; she liked to listen to his stories. When he wasn't busy being awful, she enjoyed his sense of humor.

She found him attractive, too. Maybe not classically handsome, but still . . . she liked to look at him, especially when he was unaware of her.

"You're wrong about how I feel," she told him quietly. "If *all* you can see is me looking down on you, then maybe you're not really looking."

It was his turn to appear surprised, taken aback. "Is that so?" he asked. He surveyed her face as though really taking her in for the first time. "It's possible, I suppose, that this war has hurt my eyes more than I realized."

They stared at each other for a long moment before she sat and began reading again, glad for an excuse to put her head down and conceal her expression from him. Some new emotion had taken hold of her. This new feeling was chaotic and frightening. It made her want to hide from him until she understood it better.

CHAPTER SIXTEEN
Reading Partners

Jack rubbed his eyes and then continued counting the words in *Great Expectations*. The little lamp at the table beside the upholstered chair threw only a dim light and his eyes were getting tired. He'd had sharp eyes before the gas attack burned into them. It scared him to think that they might never be as good again.

Emma rearranged her position in the large chair where she was sleeping and mumbled something. They'd spent the last three rainy days quietly reading companionably together.

Since their blow up, she'd become somehow different toward him, quiet, almost watchful. He felt changed toward her, too. He still found her beautiful and he longed to kiss her, but he no longer felt so defensive.

Now that he knew she didn't view him with contempt, he could relax in her presence. He savored her

89

words: *You're wrong about how I feel.* He heard her say them repeatedly in his mind. But he longed for more explanation. If she didn't disdain him, think him a lowly, unworthy creature, then what *did* she feel toward him? His pride, and his fear of receiving some lukewarm, evasive reply he didn't want, kept him from asking.

He had to banish these obsessive thoughts from his mind, push them aside with all his willpower. He had a task that required his full concentration, and thinking about what she might—or might not—have meant was a major distraction.

And so they had spent the quiet, rainy days finding pleasure in reading there together. At least she'd *thought* he was reading, although he was really counting the words in the book on his lap, squinting hard with his damaged eyes, concentrating on keeping track of his count. Directing himself not to think of her.

Now that she had gone to sleep, he used pencil and paper to transform the information Claudine had given him into the code. On the top of a piece of paper he wrote *Great Expectations* 85. He also wrote down the publisher of the book and what edition of it he was using. That instructed the reader to get the exact same copy of that book and turn to page 85. Then he wrote out his message by finding the letters he needed on the page. If the first letter he needed was the twentieth letter on the page, he wrote 20. If the second letter was the thirteenth letter on the page, he wrote 13, and so on. It was tedious work.

Emma mumbled again in her sleep, and he put down his pencil and turned toward her. He recalled how earlier that day she had looked up from her book and seen him with his finger under each word, moving it along as he counted. He knew she thought that he read like that, slowly, moving his finger from word to word like a child. Despite his new ease with her, it embarrassed him to have her think that. But Claudine was right: They didn't want to endanger Emma with the knowledge of what they were doing. The less she knew, the better.

CHAPTER SEVENTEEN
A Possible Escape

"You will listen carefully today," Colonel Schiller said to Emma as he helped her climb into the wagon on the next market day. "I want to know anything you hear that pertains to the war."

She nodded as two guards climbed in behind her, different ones from the time weeks before when she'd gone to the market with Willem and Claudine.

Willem snapped the reigns to move the massive horse forward. One of the guards smiled at her and she responded with a tight, perfunctory smile in return. "You do not intend to escape, do you?" he asked in German.

"Of course not," she replied, also speaking German. "There would be no place for me to go."

"That is what I thought," he said pleasantly. "It is not so unpleasant for you at the estate," he added.

"Not terribly," she agreed as the wagon rumbled on.

It was true that conditions there weren't really so bad. Each day Claudine brought up trays with whatever food the soldiers ate. She'd have liked a proper bed but she'd grown used to curling up in the chair. Now that Jack was so much better, she would ask him to take the chair some nights.

"The colonel expects you to find information for him?" the soldier, a boy with dark hair, went on. "You are aware of that, yes?"

"Yes."

"And I know why you are willing to do this," the second soldier, a tall blond, chimed in.

"Why is that?" she asked, curious to know what he thought.

"Because he will shoot you if you don't," the second soldier blurted, laughing. The first soldier jabbed him in the ribs, scowling at him for his crudeness.

He can't shoot me if I'm not there, Emma thought, angered at the insinuation that she had no choice in the matter.

Despite the fact that the soldier thought it was a joke, the threat was real. She had no new information to feed the colonel. She would be forced to learn something and hope that it was an unimportant, stale piece of information, one that would not truly jeopardize the Allied war effort. At the best, it would be tricky; at the worst, impossible.

She fingered the chain of the gold locket she now wore around her neck. Could she bribe these two soldiers by offering them the locket? Would it be enough?

They continued on without speaking. To test the possibility of bribing them, she took the locket off and opened it. She wanted to take the photo of her parents out before offering it and she also wanted to gauge their interest. The dark-haired soldier watched her as she picked at the damaged, wrinkled photograph.

"You are going to tear that if you try to lift it," he noted after watching her attempts to extract the picture. "You should leave it be."

She nodded, snapping the locket shut and returning the chain to her neck. If the picture couldn't be taken out, she wouldn't let go of it. It was all in the world she really had, at this point. She hadn't realized how much the picture meant to her until she saw it again.

"You miss your parents?" the dark-haired soldier asked.

"Very much."

He nodded in sympathy. "Me too."

In another ten minutes they arrived at the marketplace outside a small farming village. As Willem halted the carriage and helped Claudine to climb down, the blond soldier climbed forward into the driver's seat, followed by the other soldier. "We are taking your carriage to see some girls we know," the blond soldier told Willem. "We will be back for you in two hours."

"They don't understand German," Emma explained as Willem helped her down from the wagon.

"Then make them understand," the blond soldier barked at her.

Emma watched the soldiers ride off down the

road. She wasn't really too concerned about communicating the soldier's words to the couple since she didn't believe they had any intention of running off.

Behind her, the market bustled with activity. It was too early for new crops to be sold, but there were fresh eggs, root vegetables stored in cellars from the autumn before, bread and other baked goods. Normally she liked to visit the woman who created her own lavender soap, and her husband, who made creamy cheeses and yogurts from the milk their goats produced. But today she looked beyond the stalls and tables, concentrating instead on the aisles leading to the pathways into the woods.

Turning her attention from Claudine and Willem, she surveyed her surroundings. A stall selling smoked meats and fish was nearest the woods. She would buy a basket of provisions for herself, going to the smoked table last. From there, she would slip into the woods. Without the soldiers watching her, it wouldn't be too difficult.

She'd been in those woods as a child when she'd accompanied Claudine to market along with her mother. She thought she recalled a path that her mother had once told her wound all the way north toward the sea. Keeping to the woods and back roads, she'd try to follow the coastline over to Dunkirk. The Germans might have already taken control of the coast. She had no way of knowing. She might encounter enemy soldiers but she'd pose as a local farm girl and they'd have no reason to stop her. She hoped.

Willem and Claudine had gone over to a butcher they seemed to know, a tall fellow wearing a blood-splattered apron. Emma watched the welcoming delight on the big man's face as he greeted them. They obviously knew one another well. The last time they'd been to market they'd spent a long time together. She wondered how someone so seemingly jolly could spend his days among slaughtered carcasses, killing the animals himself, in all probability. But then, this war had already taught her that people were much more complex—and capable of more good and more bad—than she would ever have dreamed possible.

Emma didn't know if Claudine and Willem were being held prisoner or had simply stayed on because they had no place else to go. They'd been taking care of the estate for years and probably didn't care too much who owned it.

Scanning the crowd, she saw that uniformed German and Austrian soldiers seemed to be stationed at every aisle. What exactly were they guarding?

Taking the money Colonel Schiller had allotted her from the cloth purse she'd slung across her shoulder, she purchased a net bag from a vendor. One stall at a time, she filled it with food for her trip. When she came to the husband and wife who made the soap and cheese, she noticed that they exchanged darting, meaning-filled glances as she approached.

Emma was about to ask for a log of the goat cheese from the farmer, but instead of taking her order he beckoned surreptitiously to his wife. "You are Emma

Winthrop from the estate, yes?" the wife whispered in a German heavily inflected with Flemish.

Emma nodded.

"Our son is fighting with the Belgian army," the wife continued, leading Emma over to her soap table and pretending to show her different products. "Recently he smuggled a bag of mail to us and we are trying to deliver it to the proper people. We had a letter for you but didn't know how to deliver it with the Germans encamped in your home. They would have taken it and arrested us. They are very concerned with spies passing secrets beyond enemy lines. Most of these guards are just here to listen and observe."

"They have tried to enlist me as a spy," Emma confided, smelling one of the soaps as she spoke.

"You would never?" the wife gasped.

"No," Emma assured her. "In fact, I hope to escape down that path."

The wife reached into her apron. "I have a letter here for you. When I saw you at the market last week, I knew I would have a chance to deliver it to you." Lifting the letter from her pocket, she put it down on a wrapped bar of soap. "Take the soap and letter and drop it into your bag," she instructed.

Emma didn't dare examine the letter but she knew instantly from the elegant, formal writing that it was from her father. Did he have a plan to rescue her? She ached to rip open the letter but fought down the urge.

"Where would you go?" the wife asked.

"Dunkirk."

"On foot?"

Emma nodded.

"It's far," the wife warned, "nearly twenty-five miles. And from there you might need to go farther to the port in Calais in order to cross the Strait of Dover, because I don't know if boats are even leaving Dunkirk these days."

"I'll manage," Emma replied with more assurance than she actually felt.

"There's a better path right behind the stall. It's narrower but safer and leads to another dirt path that will take you out to a country road," the wife told her. "You can follow that all the way to the North Sea. My grandfather was a sailor and he said it was the fastest way to come back home."

"Thank you."

"Wait until my husband and I create a diversion, then go," the wife added.

Emma paid the woman for the soap and then wandered to the far corner of the stall. It wasn't long before the wife stood in front of her stall scolding her husband in Flemish. The husband, acting equally enraged, shoved her, and his wife tumbled backward onto the ground. People nearby hurried over to console the wife but she jumped back up and lunged at her husband, wrapping her hands around his throat.

Emma recognized the diversion—her chance to escape. Quickly ducking behind the stall, she walked briskly the two yards to the woods. Once inside the trees, she began to run.

CHAPTER EIGHTEEN
Love Potion

"Mam, I just can't get my strength back," Jack cried in frustration to the regal woman sitting beside him on the giant bent, twisted root at the foot of a towering cedar in the flooded forest. "Swimming in that cold well took all I'd gained out of me."

"It cost you dearly," she agreed, holding her two palms up to him as though sensing his energy. "The spirit field around your body is very weak."

"I want to be completely well again!" he shouted, burying his face in his hands in despair. The long healing process was defeating him. He was used to being vigorous, strong, and fast. He didn't recognize this injured body as his own. It angered him to be trapped inside of it.

"You've been deeply hurt," she sympathized, stroking his hair tenderly. "Your body has been ravaged with poison and your spirit has been wrung dry from seeing so much death and misery. The old healing ways can only do so much, especially when they are ministered in this dream time and in this manner."

Again she smeared the concoction of swamp mud and tree lichen across his eyes. He sighed at the wonderful coolness. His burning eyes hadn't felt this soothing relief since the last time she did it.

"Mam, I met a girl and I want her to think loving thoughts toward me. How can I make her love me, weak and wrecked as I am right now?"

"Do you love her?"

He hesitated. Did he? Really? Or was it simply pride? Did he want to know that she would see him as worthy of her love?

He thought of her curled in the chair with the lamplight falling on her brown curls; how graceful and peaceful she looked then. He remembered how her eyes flashed when she was angry with him. He recalled her bravely helping him out of the well and the vulnerability he'd seen in her face the day they had fought over which of them was the more prejudiced.

"I think I do love her," he told his mother. "But what hope can I have of winning her as I am now, low as an injured swamp frog?"

"You are no such thing," she said with a note of irritation. "You are from a line of kings and queens taken from their lands; driven from their homes, but royal just the same. My great-great-grandmother was a princess of the Natchez people, her daughter was a revered medicine woman. Many bloods have mingled with those of your ancestors since that time; they have blended to make you the fine prince that you are."

"In my world I am no prince," he scoffed.

"There are princes of your world who are more common than any peasant," she insisted. "You are a true prince of the spirit. And you have been taught the princely magic. Do not forget who you are."

As he gazed on her, she began to lose her vividness. He didn't know if it was his eyesight or if she was leaving him. "How can I make her love me?" he asked, desperate to hear her words before she was gone.

"Be always worthy of her love."

"But I am not strong as I once was," he said despondently.

"You have been taught the love potion," she replied. "It's locked in your memory, my darlin' boy. It is there for you to find. But be cautious about using it. It is the stuff of trickery and deceit. Do not use it lightly."

Once again, time speeded up and the clouds raced past. In the next second he was staring up at the rich brocade of the bed's canopy. Touching his eyes, he discovered that they had stopped burning though there was no longer any mud on them.

His mother had taught him this intentional dreaming as a young boy. It felt so real that he was never sure if he had actually transported his soul somewhere or if it was, indeed, a dream.

Back when his mother was alive, some people had claimed that they'd seen her in one place at noon and then others had sworn she'd been spotted miles away mere minutes later. Even after her death people continued to make the same claims. She was one of fifteen children, nine of them female. It was possible folks were seeing her sisters, Jack's aunts—and, later, maybe they were even seeing one of his own five older sisters. He'd been raised in a world so ripe with superstition and magic that he could never be sure of what was real and was not.

Gazing around the room, he realized that Emma had gone out. A plate of cabbage, potatoes, and sausage by his bed told him that Claudine had already been there with lunch. That's when he remembered that it was their day to go to the market.

A terrible dread washed over him like a case of cold chills. Something was not right.

He felt her absence more keenly than he ever had when she was gone, as though she'd taken every last bit of her essence and energy out of the room and was now irrevocably and absolutely gone forever.

The very idea of never seeing her again formed a cramp in the pit of his abdomen, and he curled in the bed feeling sick to his stomach. If he had been unsure before whether or not his love was genuine, he knew it now with complete certainty. Only true love lost would have the power to cause him this much pain.

CHAPTER NINETEEN
Late-Night Visitors

When Emma was about a quarter mile into the woods, she stopped to lean on a tree. Before this, she hadn't dared to rest but now she felt safe enough. More than anything, she wanted a moment to tear open the letter the woman had handed her.

My Dearest Rose and Emma,

I pray this letter reaches you both, as I am sick with worry for your safety. I shall never forgive myself for allowing you to take such an ill-conceived journey. All I can say in my defense is that the estate has always seemed to exist in an isolated world of its own and it never seemed possible that the war would reach you there. I suppose I thought of it as enjoying the same protection that those of us in England experience, at least for the moment, although that too could end if the enemy gains control of the English Channel as they are so aggressively attempting to do.

She looked up from the letter, tears filling her eyes. He *didn't* know about her mother, then. Her letter never reached him.

At least, judging from the tone of the letter, he didn't think her mother had left him. He simply believed they were stuck here together due to the war. How she wished that were true.

For the moment, though, my fondest wish is to have you both home safe with me, she continued reading. *I have attempted to come get you myself but to no avail. The several boats I have attempted to hire have cancelled the trip due to German U-boat attacks in the channel. I have succeeded in contacting a Mr. Delmont Mayhew, an associate of mine residing in Dunkirk. I have written his address at the bottom of this letter. I exhort you to reach him in that town. I have paid him handsomely to arrange your safe transport across the channel.*

How desperately I wish I could be there to comfort you. I hate to think of you both there trying to make sense of this seemingly senseless war. Keep in mind that one of the reasons we are at war now is because we must honor the promises we have made to our allies. It is an honorable thing to stand by your promises; one of the few ways we have left of knowing the right thing to do in a world that is rapidly giving way under the pressures of chaos.

Emma put down the letter, her tears now falling freely in trails down her cheeks. It was as though her father were right there, speaking to her. How deeply she wanted to wrap her arms around him and sob. "But he's not here. It's only a letter," she reminded herself as she wiped her eyes.

Lifting the letter again, the word *promise* seemed to jump off the page at her.

Her father's words made her recall her promise to Jack. If he gave her the locket, she would be his true friend. She'd said the words *I promise*. The deal was nothing if not utterly clear.

But the terms were not as obvious. She hadn't delivered the so-called friendly kiss. What held her back was the fear that he was secretly laughing at her. She could easily picture him chuckling and saying he'd received better kisses from a skeeter hawk or one of his other colorful phrases. Everything was a joke to him.

Still . . . she *had* promised to be his true friend and to kiss him, as a friend. But the truth was . . . she thought she knew what this new feeling toward him was.

Possibly it was love, or something like it. She didn't exactly know what this kind of love felt like. She'd thought she'd loved Lloyd, but she had always really known, deep down, that it had been just thrills and excitement, not really love.

But if this thing she felt toward Jack was love . . . and she kissed him . . . and he made a joke of it . . .

If that happened, she couldn't bear it.

But . . . she *had* promised to be his friend. Would a true friend leave him behind, thinking only of her own escape to Dunkirk?

"Hey there, sug. I didn't expect to see you again," Jack greeted her casually from the bed when she came into the room that evening.

"Oh? Why?" she asked, setting her net bag of foods down on the dresser.

"Just had the feelin' you were tired of being cooped up, that you might make a break for it."

"I did make a run for it, if you must know," she revealed, "but it didn't seem right to just leave you here all alone."

"It's a free world—at least last time I looked, it was," he commented breezily.

His remark made her feel like a total fool. Here she'd given up her chance to escape because of her promise to him, and he couldn't care less. Infuriated, she picked a hairbrush off the dresser and hurled it at him.

"Hey!" he shouted, dodging the brush. "I am a wounded soldier in Her Majesty's army, if you don't mind!"

"You're not even that injured anymore," she came back at him angrily. "Come to think of it, it's time you took the chair and let me have the bed."

"As you wish, princess," he said, getting off the bed.

"Don't start calling me that!"

"That's what you are, a spoiled princess, isn't it?" he said as he moved to the chair.

"I most certainly am not!"

He just sat there smirking at her in that superior way that enraged her so. Why had she ever come back for this grinning idiot, let alone had the idea that she was in love with him?

It was beyond imagining. Being shut up in this room with him was making her lose her mind!

ᕽ   ᕽ   ᕽ

That evening she stretched out on her newly returned bed to read. She'd finished *Pride and Prejudice* and had moved on to *Wuthering Heights*, by Emily Brontë. It was a story of ill-fated, turbulent romance taking place on the Scottish moors between Cathy, a young woman of means, and Heathcliff, the difficult and proud orphan her father had brought into the house. Her friends at the Hampshire School had told her it was a wonderfully tragic love story, but so far she'd just found Heathcliff to be annoying and arrogant.

Jack sat in the chair with his legs slung over the arm, still reading *Great Expectations*.

Slow reader, she observed, glancing over at him.

In another half hour he was asleep in the chair, the book in his lap, his blanket piled on the floor below him.

Watching him sleep, looking so boyishly vulnerable, caused some of her anger toward him to seep away. Maybe it was just his pride that made him act like he didn't care. She'd been so focused on her own insecurity, her fear of ridicule, that she hadn't considered he might harbor insecurities of his own. It was possible he had realized she might not come back and was only trying to cover up his feelings.

With a sigh, she got out of bed, took the book from him, and replaced the blanket. She did these things warily, half expecting his arm to snap out as it had before, but he continued to sleep, muttering something about alligators and swamp mud before settling down again.

After going into the bathroom to put on her long white nightgown and undoing the pins from her hair, she crawled into bed.

Outside the window to her left came a familiar whistling sound. She turned toward it in time to see a bright flare out in the fields. A missile had gone off. In the distance she heard the deadly *rat-tat-tat* of machine gun fire. Another battle had begun.

Pulling the pillow over her head, she shut her eyes tightly. Her nose and eyes tingled, making her expect to cry but no tears came. Maybe, she considered with some alarm, she had none left.

Emma bolted to a sitting position there in the darkness of the bedroom.

A horrible strangled sound, like someone being choked to death, had awakened her.

"Jack!" she realized, throwing off her covers and stumbling to him in the dark. Out in the fields, an exploding shell lit up the room and she saw him thrashing in the big chair.

"I'm coming! Hold on! I'm coming!" he shouted.

She sagged with relief. It was a nightmare, no doubt set off by the battle outside.

"Jack," she said, reaching to shake him. His flailing arm knocked her to the floor. "Wake up!" she shouted, grabbing hold of his leg as it kicked out, nearly hitting her in the face. "Wake up! Wake up!"

His eyes snapped open, wide with horror, larger than she'd ever seen them.

"It's okay! You're safe," she soothed him.

She saw he still wasn't sure where he was. His teeth chattered as a tremble ran through him. She settled on the arm of the chair and rubbed his shoulder. After a moment, he came fully awake and buried his face in his hands.

"Do you want to talk about it," she offered cautiously, "or would you rather not?"

He looked up at her, opened his mouth to speak, but then hesitated.

"It's all right. You don't have to protect me. I can take it," she assured him softly, though she was not entirely sure this was true.

"I dreamed I was back at the gas attack," he began. "When the gas hit, there was a kid in the trench next to me, just fifteen years old. He lied about his age to enlist. I lost sight of him durin' the attack. He was callin' to me in the haze, but I couldn't find him."

"It must have been horrible," Emma murmured.

"It was. I hope that kid made it out. If I hadn't been able to hold my breath for so long, I don't know if I would have made it out of there."

"You came a long way," she commented.

He nodded. "I just kept tryin' to find trees and water to shield me from the gas."

"Did you really sign up simply to get the uniform?" she asked.

"Naw," he said with a grim laugh. "I was just messin' with ya when I told ya that. I got swept up in the excitement of the whole thing. And I didn't think it was right that America was stayin' out of it. England is our ally, right? So you got to stick up for your friends. That's the way I saw it, anyhow."

"Awfully idealistic," she observed.

"Could be," he allowed. "Might just be awfully dumb."

"No," she disagreed, "not dumb."

"I really thought you were going to make a run for it today," he confided.

"Why did you think that?"

"I have feelin's sometimes, premonitions, I suppose. My mam had 'em too. People came to her to have her predict things. She taught me to trust those feelin's, but this time I was wrong, it appears."

"You were nearly right," she confessed. "I was about a quarter mile into the woods, but I came back."

"I guess I'm not the only idealist," he remarked seriously.

The comment made her smile wistfully. "We're some pair, eh?"

"Yeah, you right about that," he agreed, "a coupla real dopes."

Emma startled to waking. She'd fallen asleep still on the chair arm, her head resting against its back.

A strip of brilliant hall light shone in from the door. Rough orders were barked in German as three soldiers were pushed into the room.

Emma hurried to the dresser and turned on the lamp. Three soldiers stood before her. From their uniforms she saw one was French, one was Canadian, and the third, the youngest, was English.

Jack had awakened and risen from the chair. "Hey, Kid," he said cheerfully. "Nice of you to drop by. I was just talkin' about you."

A look of happy amazement appeared on the young soldier's thin, pale face. A bloody gash ran across his forehead. As he went to speak, he staggered backward, tumbling to the floor.

Jack rushed to his side. "I'll get a wet cloth from the bathroom," Emma said, hurrying off to get it.

"He just got out of the hospital where he's been since after the gas attack," the French soldier said in French. "We were sent to find out who was up here and we were caught. He fell over and hit his head on a rock when they fired at us. Luckily the bullet missed him."

Jack lifted the boy's jacket to reveal that his shirt was soaked in blood. "It didn't miss him entirely," he replied in French.

CHAPTER TWENTY
Louisiana Magic

Emma awoke the next morning, curled in the chair. After washing the boy's wounds as best they could, they'd laid him in the bed. The two other soldiers stretched out on blankets to sleep on the rug.

Jack had also slept on the floor, but he wasn't there now. The door to the bathroom stood ajar, and she craned her neck for signs of movement but all was silent inside.

Dressing quickly in the bathroom, she returned. The Canadian and French soldiers both sat with their backs against the wall. Claudine had come in with five plates and a serving bowl of oatmeal with no accompanying milk.

The German guard who had come in with Claudine barked for her to put the tray down and leave the room. She cast an apologetic look at Emma, but there was clearly nothing she could do. Before this they had been getting the same meals as the soldiers but now apparently they were to be fed prisoner's rations.

"The soldier on the bed is injured," Emma told the guard in German.

"I will tell the colonel," he replied as he left with Claudine.

A few moments later, Colonel Schiller arrived. "He's been shot," Emma told him.

"I am aware. I shot him myself," the colonel replied.

"He needs help."

Colonel Schiller glanced at the other two soldiers and then turned back to Emma. "We tended to your husband because he is not the enemy. We do not owe this soldier anything. If he dies, he dies."

The Canadian soldier swore at him, but it only made the colonel laugh. "Spies take their chances and deserve what they get," he remarked. "Speaking of which, we shall have a talk later about your recent trip to the market." He gazed around the room. "Where is your husband?"

No handy story came to her lips this time. She hadn't the slightest idea where he had gone or how he had done it. It was as though he had just vanished!

"Your husband?" Colonel Schiller pressed.

The air filled with tension as she again failed to answer. With darting eyes she looked to the soldiers for aid. Had they seen where he'd gone? With the smallest of movements, they shook their heads and lifted their eyebrows, indicating that they couldn't help.

"Ya, you right. That faucet knob is stuck tight, honey pie," Jack said, stepping out of the bathroom as if they'd been engaged all along in a dialogue regarding the plumbing. "I can't turn it either."

Emma forced herself to be bright. "See? I told you, dear."

With an annoyed cough, Colonel Schiller left. Emma immediately rushed to Jack. "Where were you?"

Without answering, he returned to the bathroom and took her net grocery bag from the linen closet, handing it to her. It contained milk and a hunk of cheese, a small round loaf of bread. The things she'd brought back from the market were already gone. These were new. Had he made a trip all the way to the market to replace them? How would that have been possible? "Where did you get these things?" she asked.

He grinned. "Louisiana magic."

"No, really?" She insisted on knowing, following him into the bedroom.

"You don't have to believe me if you don't want to," he said.

"Tell me," she demanded.

"Claudine left the back door to the kitchen open," he revealed in a reluctant whisper as he lifted a small bundle tied in cloth from the string bag.

"What's that?" she asked, coming alongside him.

As he untied the bundle a foul stench poured out of it. It reminded Emma of a dead animal decaying.

"Oh! Awful!" she cried, recoiling. "What is it?"

"It's exactly the magic that Kid, here, needs." Jack inhaled as though it were an apple pie baking, closing his eyes with delight. "Mud, lichen, and, best of all . . ." Reaching into the bag he pulled out something brown and shriveled. "Bat wing," he said, crushing it into powder over the bag's opening. "There's all sorts of good minerals and healing aids in there."

"You can't be serious!" Emma cried.

"I most certainly am serious. Do you know what a prize this is, a wonderful piece of luck? I found the poor little fella lying on the ground. My mam believed bat saliva could prevent a stroke or a heart attack. She read to me about a fella named Pliny in ancient Rome who believed that if you put bat blood under a woman's pillow at night, she'd wake up and be in love with you."

"That's ridiculous," Emma maintained.

"Is it? Mam met a man from Trinidad who swore drinking bat's blood could make you invisible."

"Ugh! How nauseating," Emma said with an expression of disgust.

He smiled at her repugnance over the bat.

"Where is the rest of the bat?" she asked.

Ignoring the question, he poured the mixture he'd made onto one of the plates and wet it with some of the milk he'd brought in. Taking scissors off the dresser, he went to sit beside the boy sleeping in the bed and snipped off a half inch of his blond bangs.

"I think you've gone mad," Emma commented as

he sprinkled the hair into the brown, reeking concoction he now cupped in his palm. She looked to the other two soldiers for confirmation of this, but they simply shrugged as they poured milk on their oatmeal.

"Wake up, Kid," Jack said, shaking the boy gently. "Doctor Magic is here to fix you up. Soon you'll be right as rain."

Almost as if his words had brought it on, thunder clouds abruptly dimmed the light. Raindrops splashed against the windows. Jack laughed, delighted. "It's what I'm sayin'—right as rain!"

The next day, the British and Canadian soldiers were taken to a separate room. Emma guessed it was her old bedroom by the direction and distance of the footsteps and the closing door. Colonel Schiller allowed Kid to stay in the room with Emma and Jack probably because they were taking care of him so well.

Astoundingly well, Emma thought with amazement as she sat in the big chair one afternoon with her copy of *Wuthering Heights* in her lap. Jack's disgusting salve applied over Kid's wound had stopped the bleeding entirely. By the next morning the injury was no more than a raised, twisting, red mark.

"It don't even hurt, Jack," Kid said now, sitting up in bed and gazing at Jack with awe and gratitude.

"Lucky thing the bullet passed right through you," Jack noted as he sat on a hard-backed chair and watched the rainstorm continue to pound the windows.

"I'm sure glad I came upon you here," Kid told

him. "Most of the guys in the fields don't run into doctors as good as you. I sure was lucky."

Jack smiled before turning his attention back to the rain-soaked window. Emma turned in the big chair and put down *Wuthering Heights* to observe him; he watched the rain as if entranced by it. What was he thinking about? Surely he was crazy as a loon.

"How are you doing this?" Emma asked him once Kid had fallen off for a nap. "How did you learn all this . . . I don't know what to call it . . . folk medicine?"

"My mam was the queen of healin' magic in our parish and she taught me all she knew," he replied.

"How are you getting out of here?" she asked.

"More magic."

"Be serious."

"Maybe I'm drinkin' bat's blood and turnin' invisible."

"Stop! I thought we were going to be friends," she reminded him. "Friends don't keep secrets."

"Sometimes they do," he disagreed. "Some secrets are too powerful to share—or too dangerous."

"I don't know if we can be friends if you feel that way," she said.

"Fine by me, sug. Truth be told, it's not only your friendship that I wanted. If I can't have your love, I can live without your friendship. Who needs it?"

"You are so arrogant!" Emma shouted at him, and then lowered her voice to a fierce whisper in deference to Kid's need to sleep. "You want me to love you? Right now, I don't even like you! I was only trying to abide by my promise, which I made only to get my locket back. Do you think I could love a superstitious fool who believes in all this nonsense magic?"

"You would love me if I wanted you to," he came back at her angrily. "Don't you think I learned to make love potions? There are more methods than the one Pliny the old Roman knew. There are hundreds of different kinds, and my mam taught them all to me."

Emma looked at him, stunned. She didn't believe him—yet she'd seen firsthand how his potion had healed Kid.

Could he really make her love him if she didn't want to? Did she believe he had that power?

Suddenly, she was unsure. "You wouldn't do that," she said uncertainly.

"No," he agreed, his anger seeming to drain away. He turned back to the window, once again staring out into the rain. "I wouldn't."

CHAPTER TWENTY-ONE
The Kid

Claudine came in to collect the plates. Emma was in the bathroom washing up, preparing to go to the market. Kid lay asleep on the bed. "Do you have it ready?" she asked Jack, speaking French.

"One second," he replied in French, checking back and forth between the numbers he'd written on his pad and the open copy of *Oliver Twist* on his lap. "How do you spell the name of the chlorine gas they use now? Is it with a *k* or a *c*?"

She didn't know, so he spelled chlorine as best he could on his pad before looking on the printed pages for the corresponding numbers he required. When translated, his sentence would read: *They are replacing the kloreen gas with a much worse one called mustard gas. They are also trying to make a gas that will eat through the rubber on the gas masks.* Emma had heard two guards discussing this one day when she happened to be standing just on the other side of the door. She'd told Jack, and now Claudine would carry this information to her friend the butcher, who would pass it on from there.

The bathroom door began to open as Jack hastily thrust the coded paper at Claudine. "You look nice, sug," he told Emma as she entered the room dressed to go to the market.

"Thanks," she grunted.

"Is your friend the colonel expecting you to bring him back some big Allied secret today?"

She sighed miserably. "I don't know what to tell him! If I hear anything useful to him I'm certainly not going to reveal it. It's not easy to keep coming up with useless facts."

"Tell him George the Fifth and Czar Nicholas and Kaiser Wilhelm are all first cousins," he suggested lightly. This fact always astounded him, that the leaders of England, Russia, and Germany were all grandchildren of England's Queen Victoria. "Tell Colonel Schiller that the royal brats have all kissed and made up, so everyone gets to go home."

She smiled wanly. "If it were only that simple," she said. "I really need something to tell him, though."

"Kid told me he heard in the trenches that Turkey is talking about joining Germany and Austria," he suggested. He figured that if Kid had heard it, the Germans knew it too, but it might sound convincing to the colonel.

She considered this and nodded. "Thanks. That

might work. I'll say I overheard two shoppers talking about it."

"Good luck," he said as she left with Claudine, "and see if you can bring back some good cheese."

"You two aren't really married, are you?" Kid asked. He was awake and looking out at Jack from beneath the covers. "I heard that colonel say you were."

"It's only a cover story," Jack replied from across the room. "Emma figured that if they didn't know I was a Brit soldier, they would be nicer to me. Since I talk American, she hoped they might believe it, and they did."

He smiled at the memory of that day as he walked toward Kid. "You should have seen her givin' it to them, all high and mighty British, tellin' them this was her place and she'd go where she pleased. You'd have thought she was the queen herself. You've got to admit that it was quick thinkin' on her part, the whole husband story. It saved my bacon, that much's certain."

"But you two love each other a lot, don't you?" Kid said. "I can see it."

"Naw, she don't love me," Jack disagreed brusquely. "Listen, Kid, I've been wantin' to tell you: I'm sorry I lost track of you that day during the gas attack."

"It's okay," Kid replied. "Everybody was running in all directions, and nobody could see a thing. Wasn't it bad luck, both of us being there and not even with our own battalion."

"Rotten luck," Jack agreed.

"Fifteen thousand soldiers were gassed, British and French troops both. Two thousand soldiers were killed by the Germans that day," Kid told him. "Some soldiers just coughed themselves to death right where they stood."

"Then I suppose we were a little lucky, after all," Jack suggested. "At least we're alive and in one piece."

"I guess so," Kid agreed. "And, do you know what? The Germans didn't even gain that much ground from the attack. They didn't really understand what they'd done, so they didn't rush in to grab the land."

"It's a crazy war," Jack commented.

"But you and Emma might have never met if it wasn't for the war," Kid pointed out. "So maybe some good came out of it, after all."

"I told you, she don't love me," Jack insisted.

"I don't know," Kid replied. "I think you're wrong."

CHAPTER TWENTY-TWO
A Night of Horror

Emma noticed that Kid's vivid blue eyes brightened every day as he grew stronger. "I knew right away you and Jack weren't married. He certainly would have told me if he had a wife as pretty as you," he said one day as she helped feed him the chicken broth Claudine had brought in.

"Thanks, Kid. What's your real name, by the way?"

"You don't want to know. It's too horrible."

"What is it?"

Kid wrinkled his nose in disgust. "Wendell," he whispered. "I hate it."

"I think it has character," Emma complimented him.

"At school they used to call me Wendy to just to make me mad. Call me Kid. Everybody calls me that. I like it much better, although I don't know if it'll still be a good name when I'm an old duffer." He laughed roughly. "If I'm so lucky as to get to be an old bloke."

123

"Why did you enlist so young, Kid?" she asked.

"The lure of steady meals and a love of adventure," he replied, smiling.

It sounded to her as though he'd been asked this many times before and this was his practiced reply. "Fair enough," she said. "You were in the gas attack?"

"Oh, it was awful," he told her. "If Jack hadn't given me his big handkerchief to put over my face, it would have been even worse. He could have used it himself, but he gave it to me. That's the sort he is. I heard him calling to me through that horrible cloud, but we couldn't find each other again."

"Are the gas attacks still going on?" she asked.

"Yes, but we've got gas masks now, and that's a help."

"Does the enemy know you've got them?"

"I 'spose so. They've got them too."

"Do you mean we're also using poison gas now?" It horrified her to think that the Allies would stoop to using something so inhumane.

"We must be using it. I've seen the enemy troops wearing the masks in battle."

"It's all too awful," she said with a shudder.

"It's not the adventure I thought it would be, that's for certain. Far from it," Kid agreed. "I've seen things that will give me the frights for the rest of my days, though I may not have too many of those, the way things are going."

"Don't say that," she chided him gently. "This will be over soon and we can all go home. We just have to hang on until then."

He laughed darkly at that. "Yeah, well, hanging on will be the trick of it, won't it?"

"Where do you suppose Jack is?" Emma wondered. "I can't imagine how he simply disappears as he does."

"He's got magic," Kid stated as if it was a well-known fact. "In the trenches he'd be there, and then be gone, then be back again with a deck of cards or something to eat. He said his mum was a sort of magic maker back in his home and that he was heir apparent, the magic prince, or some such thing."

"He's told me as much," Emma said. "But do you believe it?"

"It's the only explanation that makes sense," Kid replied. "Who knows what goes on over in America?"

"I don't believe all Americans are as peculiar as Jack is," Emma stated firmly.

Kid grinned, amused at her lofty manner. "Even though you're not really married, you two are sweet for each other, aren't you?"

"Why would you say that?" Emma cried, alarmed by his words.

"I can tell by the way you are together," he said. "I have four older sisters. When one of them got all snappish and bossy with a fella, the way you are with Jack, it always meant she had a special liking for him. And, of course, anyone can see the way Jack looks at you."

"I snap at him because I find him incredibly annoying," Emma insisted.

"So you may think, but I only know what I've seen. First comes the bickering and snapping and then romance follows. I've never experienced it myself, of course. To me it's all still very mysterious."

"What's mysterious?" Jack asked as he stepped into the room from the bathroom, soaked and rubbing his head with a towel.

"Where have you been?" Emma demanded.

He held up her bulging net bag. "Got lots of good supplies. This rain brings out the bugs, and the ground gets so soaked that the worms have to come to the surface for air. It's easy pickin's when it rains this hard."

"Bugs? Worms? What are you doing?" Emma asked.

"I need this stuff," he said, tossing the bag into a drawer of the dresser and taking out a dry pair of Emma's father's pants and a shirt.

"How are you getting out?" Emma asked, standing to make her point.

"Magic. Now you see me, now you don't!"

"Stop saying that and tell me the truth!"

"Here's a truth: I wish your father were a smaller man," he said, holding the clothing up unhappily. "I don't feel I look my best in his things. They're too baggy on me."

"Yes, well, I'm sure he wouldn't appreciate having bats, worms, and bugs in his clothing drawer."

"You know what they say," Jack said glibly as he headed into the bathroom with the dry clothing. "'War is hell.'"

Emma spun toward the door as Colonel Schiller threw it open with an unceremonious bang. "Frau Sprat, have you talent for cutting hair?" he demanded. "The soldier who usually cuts the men's hair is ill, and they are growing unkempt in appearance."

"Um . . . not really," she said. She'd never cut anyone's hair in her life.

"Your husband, perhaps?"

"Jack, you don't know how to cut hair, do you?" she called into the bathroom, switching to English.

Jack poked his head out from the bathroom door, an eager expression on his face. "Did you say hair?" he asked enthusiastically. "My granddad owned a barbershop in New Orleans. Tell him I can cut hair like an ace."

"You are well enough to do this?" Colonel Schiller inquired uncertainly. Emma had almost forgotten he could speak English.

"Yeah, you right, I am. Nearly right as rain," Jack assured him confidently. "Speaking of rain, this is some weather we're havin', huh?"

Colonel Schiller was not interested in exchanging pleasantries about the weather. He beckoned to a soldier standing guard outside the door. "Take Herr Sprat to the barbering station and get him what he needs," he told him. With a quick wink at Emma, Jack followed the soldier out of the room.

"I guess he really likes cutting hair," Kid observed with some bewilderment.

"Apparently so," Emma agreed. Jack Verde was really the strangest young man she'd ever met.

Colonel Schiller stepped closer to Emma. "Have you anything to report to me?" he asked softly.

"Only that the Allies now have gas masks," she said, remembering that Kid had told her that the Germans and Austrians already knew this. "It will make your gas attacks much less effective, won't it?"

She was relieved that he didn't scoff at her information. Maybe he, personally, hadn't been aware of it. He nodded thoughtfully. "Too much equipment is getting through to them," he muttered.

He turned abruptly to Kid. "Are the Americans resupplying you?" he asked, still speaking English.

"I haven't seen any Americans," Kid answered, looking nervous.

"That is not what I asked, idiot!" the colonel barked. "Do your weapons and gas masks and guns and food and such come from the United States?"

"I don't know," Kid answered.

Colonel Schiller yanked Kid by the arm, pulling him out of the bed. The motion wrenched his injured rib cage, and he cried out in pain. "That's where he was hurt!" Emma protested.

"He will be much more hurt than that if he doesn't tell me what I want to know," the colonel threatened. Holding Kid roughly under the arm, he dragged him out of the room.

Emma ran to the door alongside them, but it was slammed in her face and bolted. Judging from the direction of sounds in the hall, Kid was being brought to her old bedroom, where the other two soldiers probably were.

That door was slammed shut, and she cringed to hear the harsh and angry shouts that followed. Putting her hands to her ears, she pressed her forehead to the wall, trying desperately to block out the terrible sounds that continued to come from that direction.

That night Jack came in very late. He was whistling a tune she'd never heard before. "Hey, you awake, sug?" he whispered into the dark room.

"Did you have fun?" she asked bitterly from her spot on the chair.

He came over and sat on the chair arm. In the dark she could see his outline and darker shadows. "It was sort of fun," he admitted.

He held up a paper bag to her. "Those Germans have great hair. Look how much I collected."

"You kept their hair?" she asked in disgust.

"No, you don't understand," he insisted. "Hair is full of all sorts of stuff—minerals, chemicals, all like that. My mam could sniff a person's hair and tell you what that person had for lunch. She once solved a murder case and got her cousin set free by proving that a fella had been poisoned, not choked. She did it by studyin' the dead guy's hair."

"Oh, be quiet!" she shouted at him. "I don't want to hear about hair or any of your superstitious back-country nonsense!"

"Hair's not nonsense," he disagreed. "Listen, it's finally happened. The Germans sank the American ship, the *Lusitania*, just like they threatened to do. Over a thousand people died, more than one hundred of them were Americans. It's horrible, but the U.S. will come over for sure now." He got up and went to Kid's bed. "Hey, Kid," he began.

Slowly, he realized that the bed was empty. "Where'd he go?"

"You couldn't hear it?" she asked bitterly.

"Hear what?"

"How could you not hear what was going on up here?" she shouted. Somehow she blamed him, had been blaming him all night. She knew it was irrational, but somehow she'd kept hoping that he would do something, somehow make the shouting stop.

"I was down in the kitchen and they were all singin' these crazy German songs at the tops of their lungs. What should I have been hearing?" he asked, his voice growing urgent.

"I've been sitting here listening to them try to get secret information out of Kid and the other two." As she spoke, a sob choked her voice.

It had been so awful! His not being there had made it all the worse. She felt so much stronger with him near. Being there alone, listening to the anguished cries from the other room had completely rattled her. Not even the drumming rain could drown out the sounds. "They stopped about an hour ago," she continued, forcing the words out through great, heaving sobs.

Jack cursed softly, returning to her side. Settling on the chair's arm again, he put his arm around her and she continued to cry into his chest. "He's just a boy, Jack," she sobbed. "I don't even know if he's still"—she could hardly say the words—"if he's still alive."

He stroked her hair with a comforting hand. "He's alive," he said. "I can sense it. Listen, Emma. I'll find a way to help him. Just let me think on it. I'll find a way. I promise."

CHAPTER TWENTY-THREE
The Way Out

Jack moved along the secret corridor he'd discovered, feeling the dampness in the walls increase as he grew closer to the well. He hoped he wasn't too late.

After she'd finally fallen asleep he knew he had to get busy, had to hide and be ready. He couldn't let Emma down, not after finding her there so distraught and promising her he'd take action. And he had to help Kid. He'd always harbored a gnawing guilt that he'd failed Kid during the gas attack. He wouldn't fail him a second time.

The path grew narrow and he pressed himself up against it, inhaling as he squeezed through the tight space. He liked to tell Emma that he could appear and disappear at will. He'd always wondered if his mam had that ability. She sure seemed to pop up at strange times. But the truth was that as a boy on the street he'd become very resourceful at finding his way in and out of places.

Even when he'd been down in the well the first time, nearly blind and insane with pain, he had spied the narrow utility door just above the water level. It was a lifelong habit of his to be alert to exits, entrances, and possible escape hatches. He'd thought that the door must lead somewhere, unless it was only a closet, and so he'd made a mental note of it.

But it wasn't just a closet. Once he'd found the hidden way out of the bedroom, he'd discovered that the place was full of tunnels and passages. Some of them were made innocently enough when new construction was done on the place. Other passages looked like they were intended to be secret. Who knew what kinds of crazy dukes or lords were sneaking around the place way back when? The estate—strategically situated as it was on top of The Ridge—might have always had a military use, and the tunnels might have helped folks sneak out with secrets. He wondered if anyone in Emma's family was even aware of these tunnels.

He came to the door that led to the inside of the well and peered out the small window at the top of it. The dim light filtering down into the well told him dawn was breaking.

He'd heard them take out the other two soldiers early in the morning when it was still dark. Listening carefully, he and Emma had been able to hear Kid's voice until they finally heard them taking him out of the room just fifteen minutes earlier.

Cautiously, he cracked open the door, unsure of exactly where the water level would be. It stood only an inch below the bottom of the door. The water would have rushed in if the water level was higher. Maybe that didn't matter. The door at the far end of the passage would hold it back. He assumed the window was there so a person could prepare for an incoming flood.

This was how he'd gotten to Emma so fast when she'd gone down for her locket. Lucky too that he'd seen her! He hated to think about what would have happened if he hadn't.

Pulling off his boots, he jumped into the bracingly cold water. He swam the short way to the ladder. When he pulled up onto the rungs he patted his shirt pocket, checking that what he'd need was still there. It was, so he began to climb.

CHAPTER TWENTY-FOUR
Rain

Emma opened her eyes and stretched there in the big chair. A murky light told her that dawn had come, although the rain clouds let only the grayness through. Jack lay asleep in the bed, his back to her.

The only sound was that of the steadily pelting rain.

Her eyes felt salty and swollen from so much fierce crying, and her throat was dry. She arose to wash her face and get a drink.

Before going toward the bathroom, however, she heard a voice outside shout something. Who would be out in the rain and so early? Hurrying to the window, she saw figures moving along the pond.

Two soldiers were moving Kid along, their rifles pointed at him. His hands were tied behind him. They stopped so one of the soldiers could load Kid's uniform Jacket pockets with rocks.

Emma's hand flew over her mouth, which had dropped open with alarm. What were they doing?

"Jack!" she shouted to the sleeping figure on the bed. He didn't stir. "Jack!" she called again, turning away from the window toward him.

Gunfire cracked the air, making her whirl back to the sound.

"No!" she screamed, watching wide-eyed with horror as Kid slumped to the ground.

Working together, the soldiers kicked the boy into the gray, rain-rippled pond. Then they turned back for the estate.

No no no no! Her shocked mind wouldn't accept it. There still had to be some way to fix this. She flew to Jack. "They've shot Kid!" she shouted.

Why didn't he wake up? Why wasn't he responding? She yanked his blanket from him—he wasn't there at all! Pillows had been plumped beneath the blanket to make it look like his sleeping form, but he was gone! Where was he?

A sense of unreality swept over her, as though she were in a bubble where time was moving with unnatural slowness. *Where did he go? Where did he go?*

Moving dazedly back to the window, she looked out again.

There he was—standing by the pond! Wasn't he? With the torrents of rain, she couldn't be sure.

And then he was gone.

But how could he have disappeared so fast?

℘ ℘ ℘

"Claudine, I must go outside. You must get me out!"

She said it in French, then in German, and then in English, desperate to make her understand. No matter what Jack was doing out there, she couldn't stand waiting for him to return. She needed to be with him, helping him, making sure he came back safely. Together they had to help Kid. She couldn't stand not taking action.

If it had been a nice day, she might have asked Colonel Schiller to let her take a walk, as she'd done before, but how could she explain wanting to be out in a rainstorm?

Claudine's eyes flashed with comprehension as she raised a hand for Emma to wait before checking the doorway. Then she took the tray with the uneaten breakfast she had brought in and stepped out into the hallway past the soldier on guard there.

With a cry of alarm, she tripped, throwing the food at the guard at the door as she tumbled to the floor.

The soldier shouted with surprise, then wiped the eggs from his uniform in disgust. He scolded her, but she yelled right back at him, demanding something in Flemish.

The second the soldier was on the stairs, descending, Claudine jumped up and beckoned to Emma. When Emma darted into the hall, Claudine pointed toward a back staircase and Emma ran toward it. It was a servants' stairway, never used by the family. She'd nearly forgotten it existed.

At the bottom of the winding stairs she found a

coatrack with old work coats and slickers piled on top. Grabbing a hooded black slicker, she stepped out the narrow door into the driving rain.

Keeping close to the estate, she went around until she was across from the pond and the well. Then, head down, she hurried to the far side of the well and crouched as low as she could. The rain was coming down so hard that she could barely see to the pond. She'd need to go closer to look for Kid. If Jack hadn't gotten to him already, maybe she could pull him out. Was there even a chance that she wasn't too late? Probably not, but she had to try.

Staying low, she scrambled to the pond to the spot where they'd pushed Kid in. Raindrops spattered the pond's surface, making it impossible for her to see below. It was hopeless!

Looking up at the gray estate looming before her in the rain, she was overtaken with a horror of it. The place had become a prison and she couldn't stand to go back. She'd gone back only for Jack the last time she'd tried to escape. This time, she didn't know if he'd even be there if she returned.

Still crouching low, she hurried along the pond, heading for the trees. This time she was determined to head for Dunkirk and find her father's friend.

Once she had climbed over the first rock wall and reached the forest, the spring leaves dispersed the worst of the downpour somewhat, though the tapping of the rain on their surfaces was nearly deafening. At least she could see the way ahead.

Emma had moved several yards into the forest when she heard something that made her stop.

It was a low moan—a decidedly human sound.

Following its direction, she became aware of a male figure sprawled on top of a mossy boulder about another yard away. He rolled slightly, as if he'd been unconscious and was groggily struggling toward wakefulness.

Cautiously, she crept toward him. At first, she wondered if it was Jack, but quickly ascertained as she grew nearer that this person possessed a smaller frame than his.

"Kid!" she cried with a gasp when she was close enough to see him clearly.

Turning his head toward her, he forced a smile. "Hello. What are you doing here?"

"What am I . . . ?" she sputtered, climbing onto the rock. "What are *you* doing here? I saw them shoot you and kick you into the pond."

"Then it's true," he said. "I've been lying here wondering what's real and what I only dreamed."

"How did you get out of the pond?" Emma asked, taking off her slicker and draping it over him. The boy shivered, completely soaked, his shirt plastered to his wet body by blood as well as rain.

"It might sound crazy," he replied, his voice thin and weak, "but as I was sinking down, I swear I saw a giant frog swim up from the bottom of the pond and grab me. It might have been a dream. That's all I remember, until right now. I don't know how I got here."

"It's not crazy," she told him. "I saw a creature like that in the well one time."

"What do you think it is?"

"I don't know. It was dark. I couldn't really see it." He moaned in pain, making her look down at him sharply. "Where did they shoot you?"

He attempted a bitter smile but succeeded only in twitching his pale lips. "They got me in the other side, my good side." Slowly he pushed away his jacket and touched the most blood-soaked area of his shirt.

Emma swallowed hard and forced her nerves to stay steady as she gingerly lifted his shirt, tugging gently in the places where the bloody wetness had made it adhere to his skin. "Oh my God!" she gasped when she saw the wound.

"That bad, is it?" Kid asked.

"No, it's not that! It appears that it *was* bad, but it's been tended to," she told him. A pile of leaves was pressed into a plaster of mud over the wound in Kid's side. Gazing at the dripping leaves around her, she realized she didn't see this sort of leaf anywhere. Carefully lifting the leaves, she inspected the mud. She cried out, recoiling as a worm crawled from the mound. As she caught her breath she saw that it was sprinkled with fine threads. *No, not threads*, she thought. *It's hair!*

"It's Jack," she told Kid. "He did this."

"Are you saying Jack's the giant frog?" Kid asked.

"I don't know," Emma admitted. "It's crazy. I don't know."

140

CHAPTER TWENTY-FIVE
A Secret Meeting

"We will take very good care of him," the farmer assured Emma, speaking French. He handed her a cup of tea as she sat covered by a blanket, finally starting to feel warm again.

Emma had walked for nearly three miles in the rain before she came to this farmhouse to ask for help. The Belgian farmer and his wife immediately sent their two sons to find Kid and bring him back. Once there, they had washed him and changed him into dry clothing. "Shall I wash away this mud patch?" the wife had asked.

"No," Emma had said. "I think you should leave it. The person who put it there knows about healing. He helped heal him once before."

"Very well," the wife had agreed.

Kid now lay sleeping in a soft bed. "When the flooding stops on the road, we will try to find an

Allied regiment and get him to an army hospital," the farmer continued.

"Is that possible?" she asked hopefully.

The man shook his hand back and forth. "Yes and no," he replied. "We are on the front line of the fighting here. The Allies are to the left of us, the Germans and Austrians on the right. Some days the Allies gain ground, other days they are pushed back. Some days it's only a matter of miles, even yards."

"What side are we on now?" she asked.

"You're in luck. Yesterday the Germans held this road. Today the Allies took it from them. But it could change again tomorrow. Both sides are determined to hold this area. The Allies will do whatever it takes to keep the enemy from gaining the ports at Dunkirk and Calais."

"If they control those, they can easily attack England," Emma said softly as the possibility of her country being invaded washed over her.

"I'm sure that is what they intend," the farmer agreed. "The Allies are planning a major effort to push them back even farther, but no one knows when it will come."

"Listen, you must get word to someone in charge that the Germans are at the estate up on The Ridge. They sent three soldiers up to find out. All three were captured. The soldier you are tending is one of them. They need to know that the Germans can easily see them coming from up there if they advance across the open fields. They have over a hundred soldiers there right now and are well stocked with munitions and food."

"We will tell them when we get your friend to a hospital," the farmer agreed. "But the road will soon be washed out. I can't say when that will be, but as soon as it is possible, one of the boys and I will go."

The wife came out of the bedroom with dry clothing and a towel for Emma. "Thanks, but there's no sense in changing," she declined, getting up from her chair. "I must return."

"Why go back?" the woman asked.

She'd had no intention of going back, but as she had been speaking to the farmer, the possible repercussions of her disappearance had occurred to her. "The Germans won't miss Kid because they think he's dead," she explained. "But Colonel Schiller might send someone to come after me. He won't want me telling the Allies how well fortified they are up on The Ridge. I don't want them to track me down and find Kid—or all of you. I have to go back."

"You are a brave patriot," the wife commended her.

"I just want to have a home to return to," Emma said, brushing aside the compliment as she put her slicker back on. "I'd like to say good-bye to my friend, if you don't mind."

She went to the bedroom where Kid was sleeping. His eyes opened as soon as she entered, however. Smiling softly at him, she sat at the edge of the bed. "They're going to take you to the hospital when they can, so you'll be better soon."

"You're not coming?"

"No. I don't want them out here looking for me."

He nodded, apparently understanding. "Tell Jack I'll never forget what he did for me—even if he is a big magic frog. I told you he was the best. You're right to be in love with him."

"But I'm not in love with him."

"Sure you are," he insisted quietly.

"How could I love a frog?" she said, trying to make a joke of it.

"You could do worse," he maintained as he nodded off to sleep again. Stroking his hair fondly, she padded softly from the room and prepared to leave.

Emma was glad of the riding lessons she'd taken at the Hampshire School when she was offered the use of one of the farm's horses, a gray mare named Poppy. "There's a trail through the forest about a mile down the road," one of the sons told her as he led the horse out of the barn. "It cuts through the forest in about two miles before turning around again. You can get off there and it will be only a short walk to the other side of the trees. Give her rump a slap when you dismount and she'll follow the path the rest of the way home on her own. I'll come out to fetch her in an hour or so. Poppy's a good horse, sure-footed in the mud, and nothing spooks her."

"I'm so grateful to you and your family," Emma said as she put her boot in the stirrup and pulled herself into the saddle. "Thank you."

Poppy was as easy to ride as the boy had said and didn't seem to mind the rain. The trip was so much easier than it had been on foot. Soon she saw the bend in the road and pulled to a halt and dismounted. "Go home, Poppy," she commanded, slapping the horse's rump.

She stood a moment and watched the horse gallop down the rain-soaked path. Then, gazing around, she wondered if Jack was still out in the forest.

It was good weather for a frog.

The farmer's son had been right: It didn't take her long from there to make her way back to the estate. As she emerged from the trees, she noticed one wet guard stationed on the roof of the estate. The rain had let up a bit and was not as good a cover as it had been when she left. Not knowing how to avoid him, she grabbed a handful of early poppies with fat orange buds not yet in full bloom. Draping them in her arms, she snapped a few branches of budding yellow forsythia from a nearby bush to add to her bouquet and then walked out in plain sight, continuing to pick wildflowers and even waving up to the guard. She hoped he would assume the colonel had given her leave to go out to pick flowers in the rain.

The guard waved back and didn't seem alarmed by her presence. She forced herself to stoop for flowers along the way and not betray the urgency she felt to rush to her room to check for Jack. She needed to know that he was there and safe. And she had so many questions to ask him.

Inside the servants' doorway, she returned the soaking black slicker to the rack and hurried up the stairs. Peeking down the hall, she saw a young soldier, probably no more than her own age, maybe younger, standing guard in front of her door.

Deciding that the direct approach was once again her only recourse, she strode confidently forward, thrusting the flowers toward the guard. "Here are the flowers I was sent to get," she said haughtily in German. "Tell Colonel Schiller I am not his servant and from now on he can send someone else to collect flowers if he wishes to have them."

The guard stared at her, flabbergasted, as he clutched the flowers. "I thought you were within the room all this time!" he blurted.

"I should have been, on a day like this," she replied angrily. "No. I was sent out right after breakfast and have been in the pouring rain all this time. Tell the colonel that if I fall ill with pneumonia, it is he whom I will hold responsible. Now if you will please stand aside, I need to change these wet clothes."

The soldier, abashed and confused, obediently moved to let her into the room. Once inside, she sighed with relief. "Jack?" she called softly, moving forward. "Jack?"

She crept slowly toward the back of the room. Maybe it was the dismal gray light suffusing the room, but a sudden uneasiness struck her. It seemed eerily quiet, the only sound being the ceaseless drone of steady rain.

Hovering near the open bathroom door, she turned in a half circle, and then gasped sharply as a hand wrapped her wrist in its grip.

"Shh!" Jack hissed. "Follow me." He pulled her into the bathroom closet. "Where were you?" he asked in a sharp whisper. "I was worried!"

"*You* were worried?" she whispered back irately. "You disappeared first!"

"I got Kid," he told her as he began taking items off the closet shelves and tossing them aside.

She wasn't sure what he was doing, but she helped him just the same. "I know you did," she replied.

His brows shot up in surprise. "You know?"

She nodded.

"He's okay," they both spoke at once. "I know," they said at the same time, their voices overlapping

He shot her a disgruntled, perplexed look. "Let's talk about it later. Are you okay?"

"Yes. You?"

"Fine," he answered as he finished pulling down the closet's shelving and swung open a panel behind it. It led out to a passage with floors and walls of wooden planks. "Hurry," he urged her. "But be quiet."

The passage led them to a spot above the second floor library. She could tell because spaces in the loose planking enabled her to see down into the room through a crack in the ceiling, probably a spot where the reverberations from the bombings had caused the plaster to come loose as it had in the bedroom. The words of Colonel Schiller speaking to some other officers she had never seen before floated up through the opening.

"The staff officers arrived this morning," Jack told her. "What are they saying?"

Dropping flat onto her stomach, Emma put her ear to the opening, listened carefully, and began to translate for Jack.

"You learned nothing from the captured soldiers?" one officer asked Colonel Schiller.

"No, sir. I don't believe they knew much. We shot all three of them this morning," he answered with a matter-of-fact tone.

Emma and Jack looked at each other sharply. Emma had assumed this was what had happened, but to hear Colonel Schiller mention it so coldly sent a chill through her. She saw that a pallor had swept over Jack as well.

"It made no sense to keep them here when they were no use to us," Colonel Schiller went on. "We could not release them since they had already seen too much of our operation here."

"A wise decision," another of the officers commended him. "What of the American couple?"

Again, Emma's gaze shot up to meet Jack's. Together they lowered their heads closer to the opening.

"The wife is English and speaks fluent French and German. I have allowed her to accompany her caretakers to the market to spy for us," Colonel Schiller informed him.

"Why would she be willing to do this?" the officer asked skeptically.

"I have threatened to shoot her."

"It's too risky," the first officer who had spoken objected. "How do you know she won't pass information the other way?"

"I send guards to watch them."

"Don't do it anymore," the second officer commanded. "She no doubt realizes that they will never leave here alive, so what does she have to lose?"

Emma sent Jack a darting look filled with fear. It hadn't occurred to her that the Germans didn't intend to let them go eventually. He returned her glance, but his expression remained calm. She hoped there was a good reason why he wasn't more disturbed by this news.

"Has the wife given you any valuable information thus far?" the second officer asked Colonel Schiller.

"Not really," he replied. Emma was let down at his words. She'd hoped that the gas mask news had impressed him; apparently it hadn't. At least she hadn't accidentally shared anything important.

"Why haven't you shot them already?" the first officer inquired, rising and pacing the room.

"It didn't seem prudent to shoot Americans needlessly at this time with the current political situation," the colonel explained.

"You may be right about that," the pacing officer

agreed. "Our sinking of the *Lusitania* has not been good for our relationship with the Americans. It is bad enough that they send supplies to the Allies, we do not need them sending fresh troops in addition."

"But it is only two people," the second officer pointed out, "and no one need know. They would be two less mouths to feed."

The pacing officer stopped moving and considered this. "These things get out sometimes. Right now, leave them as they are, but if the Americans declare war, then shoot them right away," he decided.

"I will do it myself at the very moment I hear," Colonel Schiller agreed.

Alarmed, Emma once again looked up at Jack. He drew a deep breath and let it out slowly. She could read his expression precisely: It said, *I told you not to trust Schiller.*

The staff officers continued to talk to Colonel Schiller about their battle plans. Through their spy network they had learned that the Allies were planning a major offensive to take The Ridge in mid June. Although the Germans and Austrians felt they were not properly equipped to win such a battle at the moment, they were satisfied that they'd be able to move in enough men and equipment by early June to win a decisive victory.

"They will put all their resources into this offensive, but we will defeat them. Then the entire North Sea corridor will be ours; a perfect gateway from which to launch our invasion of England," said the officer, who had to pace once again.

"Are you sure that they will wait until mid June?" Colonel Schiller asked. "They won't move sooner?"

"No, they won't come in this rain. The Belgians will tell them that this mud can swallow a man right down. They saw it happen last year; entire regiments drowned in the mud. These rains usually don't abate until the end of the month, and this year the local farmers are expecting the heaviest rainfall in the last ten years."

A drop of water fell onto the desk around which they sat.

Emma realized her hair was dripping.

The officers looked up to the opening.

Jack and Emma froze, barely daring to breathe.

"The roof must be leaking," Colonel Schiller surmised. "This old estate is as creaky as a sinking ship." The officers chuckled at this and together rose to leave.

Emma didn't move a muscle until she heard the door below her shut. "Is this how you've been getting out?" she asked.

He nodded.

She still didn't entirely understand how he was doing it. The opening they were in had pipes along the ceiling and had no doubt been constructed to conceal the plumbing when her mother had the new bathroom added. But they were on the third floor, so how was he escaping?

He indicated for her to follow him down the passage farther. It ended abruptly, dropping off into some kind of stone shaft. Looking up, she saw that it went up as well as down. "It's the chimney from the old fireplace in the kitchen," he whispered. "It's boarded up, but I cut a hole big enough to get out. Claudine's seen me scoot out from behind the board, but she's not tellin'."

"How do you get down?"

"I climb."

She gazed down with a shiver. "If you fell, it would be three floors. You might be killed."

"I'm real careful."

How was he getting into the well or the pond, if he was in fact the frog-man Kid and she had seen? This was a question that would be more difficult to ask. She didn't think he would admit to being a frog.

They returned back through the passage to the bathroom. When they were through the closet opening, Jack replaced the panel with the shelving. Emma stepped out of the bathroom and into the bedroom just as Colonel Schiller walked in, looking angry. "My soldier informs me that you were outside picking flowers," he barked. "I did not give you permission to do this."

"I thought you and your men would appreciate the flowers," she replied. She answered in English and spoke loudly, wanting to alert Jack to the colonel's presence.

"I suggested that they would enjoy them," Jack added, coming out beside Emma. "When I was cuttin' their hair they complained to me that the place was dreary."

"Neither of you will go anywhere without consulting me," the colonel said angrily, speaking in English. "From now on the door will be locked, the guard will be doubled, and a soldier will bring in your meals. Is that understood?"

"Perfectly," Jack said.

CHAPTER TWENTY-SIX
Darkness

After she'd told him of the day's events, of how she'd gotten Kid to safety, she'd wanted to know how he'd gotten to Kid. Jack was amazed to hear her come straight out and ask if his magic gave him the ability to turn into a frog.

"You think I'm a frog?" he asked, laughing incredulously as he stretched out on the bed.

Emma sat on the chair and faced him. "You saved me from the well. And you saved Kid from the pond. I know you did! I saw one of your crazy cures on his side."

"That doesn't make me a frog."

"We both saw something large swim up at us from below."

"I told you, I'm a great swimmer. And I have my ways of gettin' around. Why don't you let it be and stop asking so many questions?"

"Why must you be so mysterious and strange?"

He shrugged his shoulders and grinned. He enjoyed teasing her. "It's my nature, I 'spose. I probably get it from my mam. She made some folks nervous too."

"How'd she die?" Emma asked.

"Caught the malaria while she was tending to sick folk in the swamps. She told me what to do for her, but there was a couple of ingredients I couldn't find in time." He looked away from Emma. He never liked remembering how he had scrambled to find the things she told him to get and couldn't. "It's somethin' I still feel real bad about, though I know she forgives me."

And he did know. "When I'm dreamin', I sometimes try to direct my spirit to her spirit. We talk. She helps me with cures and the like. It's not easy to explain. She helped me to get better from the gas."

He himself didn't know if these were dreams or if his spirit really transported. The dreams felt so real and he had gotten much better after each time he dreamed his mother had worked a cure on him.

"You're lucky to know you're forgiven," Emma said softly, and explained how her mother had died in the attack. "I couldn't help my mother when she needed me. I wish I knew that she forgave me."

"There was nothing for her to forgive. It wasn't your fault."

"I know," Emma said as tears overfilled her eyes, spilling down her cheek. "Still . . . it feels as though there should have been something I could have done."

"There wasn't," he assured her, "there was not a thing you could have done."

"I'd really love to see my father again, and now I'm so frightened that they'll shoot us before that happens. Or maybe he'll be shot, you know, if they attack England. Maybe we'll all—" Unable to go on, she buried her face in her hands as tears rushed forward.

He came and perched on the chair beside her, rubbing her back. "You cry, Em. Go ahead," he said. "It'll do you good."

Nodding, she buried her tear-drenched face into his chest. With a sigh, he stroked her soft hair and let her weep there. Somehow he knew that these tears were touching him more deeply than even her kiss would have.

That night he pretended to sleep in the chair, listening to her breathing over on the bed, waiting to be sure she was asleep. The rain continued to pound down, making it hard to hear. Not even moonlight lightened the complete darkness.

Just when he was sure she was asleep, she surprised him by sitting up and crossing in the dark to him. "We have to get out of here and tell someone at Allied command what we heard today," she said.

"We *don't* have to go," he disagreed. "I've been sitting here thinking about it all this time. The world's gone insane. I was insane myself to sign up. All we have to do is survive until this ends."

It was only part of what he'd been thinking.

Despite the insanity he planned to go and tell what he knew, but he had to go alone. If he reported the information to the Allies and returned in time before he was missed, that would be best. He'd travel faster without her, and she'd be safer here. He might have to travel far, and the rain was torrential. He wasn't sure how much territory the Germans had claimed; he couldn't know for sure which direction was best.

But he couldn't tell her. She'd insist on going with him.

"How can you say that?" she questioned. "Don't you feel any loyalty to your fellow soldiers?"

"You haven't seen the things I've seen, Em. Things I don't want to talk about because if I tell you it'll give you nightmares for the rest of your life, the kind of nightmares I'm going to have forever. This war has changed me for always." That much was absolutely true.

"We can't sit here and do nothing," she objected.

"Sure we can," he disagreed. "What's to stop us?"

"It's wrong not to try," she insisted.

"Who says? It seems to me there's a wrong thing happen' every second of every day right now. Who cares if we do a wrong thing?"

She rose indignantly. "Do what you please. I have to try to get word to someone." She gathered her clothing and began pulling things on over her nightgown.

In her top dresser drawer, she searched in the dark until she found the locket and put it around her neck. "This time I won't be back," she told him.

"There are two guards at the door. How do you plan to get out?" he asked.

"I'll go down the chimney like you do."

"Have you ever climbed down a rock wall before?"

"I can do it."

"In those high-heeled boots?" he scoffed. "And I wouldn't recommend doin' it barefoot, either."

"I'll find a way," she said.

"Listen, Emma," he said, gripping her arm. "You're goin' to get killed out there. I'm tellin' you, don't do it. What if I go and you stay here?"

"Then we both go together," she suggested.

"No," he insisted.

She shook his hand off. "I'm going. I don't care if you want me to or not!"

"Stubborn idiot!" he cried, walking away from her toward the bathroom.

He'd hoped to slip away once he knew she was asleep. Now she was acting exactly as he'd expected she would. Fortunately, he'd prepared for this possibility and knew what he'd have to do—as much as he hated to do it.

"Do you think that just because your life in London was safe that nothing can hurt you now?" he argued, turning toward her.

"What do you know about my life?" she came back at him, furious. "At least I've been taught values like loyalty and patriotism. What would a swamp rat like you know about that?"

"Nothing!" he replied coldly. "Nothing at all! I

guess someday I'll have to go ask the queen."

She followed him into the bathroom and turned on a dim nightlight. She pulled open the closet and began pulling out the shelves.

"Hey, Em." Jack came silently behind her. He really hated doing this.

She turned around to him. He held his palm flat out horizontally, tipping it up to her. It was filled with a grayish powder, a concoction he'd made from a bat's wing and other ingredients for just this moment, should it prove unavoidable.

"What?" she asked, annoyed, as he blew the powder into her face.

CHAPTER TWENTY-SEVEN
Fire

Emma awoke and realized she was lying on the bed, on top of the covers, still dressed in her clothing, even her boots. Blinking in the dark, it took her a moment to recall what had happened but, when she did, she sat up quickly. She turned on the light at her bedside.

Outside in the hall, she heard soldiers speaking German to one another. Beyond the windows was the incessant pounding of rain. But Jack was not in the chair, and she didn't detect any sound of him moving anywhere in the bathroom.

A note propped against the lamp base caught her attention. It was a rhyme:

Jack Sprat's a real swamp rat

But on his wife he would not lean.

He ran away

So safe she'd stay

While he went to scare the queen.

"To scare the queen?" Emma pondered the meaning of his words. Did he mean he'd gone to tell the Allies the bad news? It would scare them, but of course they needed to know.

She continued to read:

Did Jack the rat

Climb out like that?

No, he acted like a hedgehog.

But have no fear—

He'll persevere

Through the muddy bog.

It's no problem for him

If he must, he'll swim

For he's not a rat or hedgehog

—he's a frog!

A breeze chilled her, and she saw that the bottom of the window had been opened just enough for a man Jack's size to slip through. Several knotted bedroom sheets had been tied together and fastened to the dresser at one end. The other end had been passed through the window opening.

Emma pocketed the note and got out of bed. She went to the window for a closer inspection. Peering out, she saw the white sheet bouncing in the rainy wind along the outside wall. Had he taken it all the way to the bottom? Why would he do that and risk being seen when he could go down the old chimney?

The bedroom door flew open, flooding the room with light from the hall as Colonel Schiller stomped in flanked by the two guards who had been stationed at the door. "Frau Sprat!" he barked. "Where is your husband?"

"He won't get far," Colonel Schiller said with a smirk on his face. He stood by the open window and sneered down at Emma as she sat on the big chair. The soaked line of bedsheet had been hauled in and now lay coiled, making puddles on the floor.

"He will, no doubt, head north to the other side of the forest. Our men regained that farm road only yesterday. I've sent a soldier with a message to our field commander there to look for him. Our troops will pick him up. And if he stays off the road, he'll wish he hadn't."

"Why is that?" Emma asked tensely.

"The mud in the fields out there will swallow him whole. The farmers have already lost sheep and pigs into it. It nearly engulfed an entire ambulance yesterday. It will suck him right into the ground. You had better hope we pick him up first."

"Will they bring him back here?" she asked.

"Yes, and then we will shoot him."

Emma leaped up from the chair. "No! Why? You can't blame him for wanting to escape from this prison. It's my fault. We quarreled terribly. I said cruel things to him. He was simply desperate to get away from me."

"A lovely performance, Fräulein Winthrop, but I know better."

"That was my name before I was married," Emma attempted to cover. "But now—"

"It was a pleasant joke, I am sure," Colonel Schiller interrupted. "I do not like to be made a fool of, however. We intercepted this bag of mail being smuggled in by a captured Belgian soldier. In it we found this letter addressed right here to the estate."

He took a letter from inside his jacket and Emma instantly recognized her father's neat, curved handwriting. It had been torn open along the top. "That's mine," she insisted, reaching for it. "Give it to me, please."

He handed her the letter. She scanned it quickly. It was full of encouragement so loving that it nearly brought tears to her eyes.

"He says that he hopes you will all live to see happier days, like your wedding day, perhaps," the colonel pointed out.

"My husband and I eloped," Emma told him, but he simply raised a dismissive hand to her and she knew he didn't believe it. "All right, we're not married, but Jack is an American and you can't just shoot Americans for no reason."

"We can do what we like to spies for any reason," he countered.

"He's no spy!"

"He is a spy. And so are you!"

He took a folded paper from his pocket and handed it to her. "One of our informants works for a butcher at the market. I assume you gave him this on your last day out." Before she had even completely unfolded the paper she saw that it mentioned *Oliver Twist*. "I don't know what this is," she said.

"I suppose those numbers mean nothing to you?" Colonel Schiller said skeptically. "Please, Fräulein, do not insult me further."

She gazed down at the line of numbers. "Is this some sort of code?" she asked.

Colonel Schiller's face began to color with fury. "Do not pretend that you do not recognize this book code. You know very well that each number signifies a letter on the designated page. Your hand is clearly in this. You brought this book from the library downstairs, did you not?"

"I had nothing to do with this. Why do you think it even came from this room? I can't work this message out," she insisted. "What does it say?"

"It says too much about my men and how we are supplied!" he shouted, pounding his hand on the dresser with rage.

Emma began to understand what had been happening. Jack had been going outside and learning things about the fortifications the Germans were bringing in: the cars, tanks, munitions, extra food, even the reinforcements of soldiers who were arriving daily. He probably even saw things when he was downstairs cutting hair. Claudine and Willem knew things too.

Then he wrote what they collectively knew, using the pages of the book as some kind of code template. He got the coded message to Claudine when she brought the meals. Claudine and Willem then passed it on to their friend the butcher, the man she'd seen them talking to at the market. He must have had some way of passing it on from there.

Slow reader. She cringed remembering how she'd passed that judgment on him. All the terrible things she'd said to him tonight, accusing him of indifference, of cowardice—it killed her now to remember them. What a fool he must have thought she was! A snobbish fool!

Emma heard talking in the hallway, and one of the guards came quickly into the room. One of the staff officers from the day before was downstairs requesting to see Colonel Schiller. Scowling at her as he turned to go, he slammed the door behind him.

Emma took the rhyme from her pocket. *Did Jack the rat climb out like that? No, he acted like a hedgehog.*

She understood! He was telling her that the window setup had been to mislead the Germans into thinking he'd gone out that way. As long as they thought that, they wouldn't search any further for a way out.

But he'd really taken the passageway out. That was what hedgehogs did, they moved through underground tunnels. This passage, although not underground, was a tunnel. He was telling her that she could still use it if she needed to.

She did need to use the passage—as quickly as possible too. She had to catch up with Jack before he became bogged down in one of those fields.

Glancing at the clock on the dresser, she saw that only forty minutes had passed since she'd attempted to leave. If she took the horse path, she might make faster progress than he did and maybe she could catch up to him. She could at least warn him not to go out into the mud that was sure to suck him down and swallow him whole.

Emma stood on the edge of the dark passage behind the wall and struck a match. The stone of the chimney flue lit up before her. Lighting the lantern she'd brought in, she hung it on a nail jutting from one of the thick wooden beams.

She had brought along the same knotted rope sheet Jack had used to fake his escape out the window. This time, she hoped, it would really do the job. She fastened it around the beam, tying it firmly. The other end, she tied around her waist. She'd attempt to climb down the chimney flue shaft as Jack had done, but this would give her some added safety should she slip.

"Here goes," she murmured, lowering herself into the black pit. Inch by tenuous inch, handhold by tense handhold, groping in the dim light for the next spot to place her foot, she slowly descended. At first, the light from the lantern was sufficient but as she went farther from it, her progress became increasingly difficult.

Her fingers were soon scraped and raw. Her shoulder muscles ached with the strain. But she kept descending, determined to put the misery out of her mind.

Several feet lower she cried out in pain. A twisting cramp clenched the muscles from the arch of her foot and ran up her calf muscle. The sudden spasm caught her by surprise and she lost her grasp on the wall. In seconds she was tumbling down the dark shaft.

Then she bounced up again, letting out a gasp of shocked air. The sheet held her swinging there, feet and arms dangling like a puppet.

With a terrible tearing sound, it dropped her several more feet. She braced for the impact. But the tear wasn't complete, and the sheet rope held for a while longer at least.

Below, she heard soldiers speaking loudly in the kitchen. Light seeped through the boarded area. She was only about twelve feet from the bottom.

Kicking out, she was able to touch the sides of the chimney with her toes. By rocking harder still, she reached the wall again. With one hand, she untied the sheet from her waist and continued the slow climb down.

Once at the bottom, she saw that her way out was blocked by the presence of the soldiers carousing in the kitchen. She didn't have the luxury of waiting. Although she'd plumped some pillows under the blanket to look like her sleeping body and shut the lights, she couldn't be certain Colonel Schiller wouldn't return, demanding to speak with her. And if she waited too long, she'd never catch up to Jack.

She paced in a small circle, not knowing what she should do next.

"They have rats in this place," one of the German soldiers declared. "You can hear them running through the walls!"

Emma froze. She hoped he was referring to the noise she was making and not to any actual rats.

In the darkness she realized that an even darker shape was behind her. With hands extended, she felt her way to it. It was a hole, a break in the stones of what must have once been the back wall of the fireplace.

Forcing herself not to think about rats, she climbed through the opening. It led to a wide, turning tunnel with a dirt floor. In places there were pieces of stone, as though this was some very old part of the estate and these had once been wide, winding stone steps.

Emma followed it down to a vast underground room filled with bottles. Lifting one from a shelf, she blew dust from it. The label said it was wine that had been bottled in 1760. She wondered when anyone had last been down here. She'd never heard her parents speak of it.

On the wall was an unlit torch in a holder. Taking it down, she lit it and began searching for some way out. Before long, she found a door and stepped through it.

Once inside, she shivered. Was it some kind of room for storing wine at an even colder temperature? With the torchlight to guide her, she crept farther into the narrow room. It wasn't long before she arrived at another door. There was a small window at the top of it. She peered through it out into darkness, but then realized that there were drops of water on the other side of the window.

Leaning forward, she put her ear to the door.

Rain falling into water?

Why would there be water on the other side of this door? But if she could hear rain, it meant she had found a way out.

Carefully, she pulled the door inward. Water lapped at the toes of her boots. She was standing right at water level inside the well.

Holding the torch high, she saw that the ladder was on the other side of the wall. Getting to it meant plunging into the rain-rippled well water.

"It's going to be cold," she whimpered as she stepped out into it. The light sputtered into darkness as the torch hit the water. Floundering, shocked by the icy chill, she splashed across until her hand finally gripped a rung of the ladder.

A rung at a time, she climbed up. Her mind raced. What should she do next? How could she get out of this well without being seen right away by a guard? They were looking for Jack, so there would be soldiers all around.

When she had climbed to just below the top of

the well, she still had no plan but she was distracted from her thoughts by a strange glow filtering down to her from outside. It almost looked like dawn, though it was too soon for that.

Soldiers were shouting to one another in German.

And she smelled something unpleasant.

Had the Allies attacked unexpectedly?

She stretched up to see just over the top of the well.

Her hand clapped over her mouth to stop herself from crying out in alarm.

Flames roared out from her parents' bedroom window. The library below it and the kitchen, too, were also engulfed in flames. The rain wasn't even enough to quench the inferno that roared out the window and shot up from the roof.

Her first thought was the lantern. She'd left it burning inside the wall. If it had fallen and set the sheet rope on fire, it would have traveled past the library and right down to the kitchen. It probably burned behind there until it was so hot that the walls burst into flames.

The realization that she might have destroyed the family's ancient manor sent a chill through her. She couldn't think of it now. It might be bombed to the ground soon, anyway. Who could tell anymore? Anything might happen. At least this way it would help her to escape.

Soldiers poured out of the house into the rain.

She recognized Colonel Schiller's voice yelling, ordering his men to carry away the crates and burlap bags of munitions stacked against the outside wall of the estate.

Emma didn't wait to see what would happen next. Climbing out of the well, she ran across the wet grass toward the forest.

CHAPTER TWENTY-EIGHT
Mud

At least the rain's finally stopped, Jack noticed as he reached the edge of the dripping forest. Out on the farm road, just beyond the trees, muddy water several inches deep gushed along like a river.

He ducked back under the cover of the trees when two headlights appeared on the road. Someone inside the car was sweeping a light from side to side, searching. In the light he saw that they were German soldiers.

Where they looking for him?

It was certainly possible.

The road would not be safe. He was clearly still behind enemy lines. It might be wiser to stay to the fields. The night was so dark, he could cut right across. With this black night to cover him, he could probably cover miles before dawn.

Until being gassed with the French troops, he'd

been stationed with the British Fourth Army some-where northwest of here. They might still be around there. He'd head west before turning north later.

Of course, it wouldn't be easy crossing these fields in their current condition. He'd have to look for rocky sections and elevated patches as much as he could. "Ah, what's a little mud to a frog like me," he said, covering his anxiety as he stepped out of the forest and into the field.

His foot instantly sank up to his calf into the soggy earth. He was forced to use both hands to yank it out and was nervous about his next step.

He saw a line of rocks. *That's it!* he thought, elated. He leaped to the closest one, and then to the next. Hopping from rock to rock would allow him to get across the field without sinking into the mud.

He kept going, trying not to worry too much about what he would do if the trail of rocks ended. In that case he could go back the same way he had come and hope to pick up another trail of rocks, but it would cost him precious time.

But what other choice did he have?

Even if he wasn't moving in the most efficient way, at least he was making a distance between him-self and the estate.

And Emma.

As he moved deftly from rock to rock, he won-dered what she was doing. If they were in fact look-ing for him, it meant they had already discovered he was gone. What would that mean for her?

A strange light was coming from somewhere. Was a battle going on somewhere? *Boy, the minute the rain stops, they start right to it again*, he thought, shaking his head bitterly.

He realized, after a moment more, that the glow was coming from The Ridge.

And then he heard an explosion up there, and the light grew even brighter.

What was going on?

Was Emma in danger?

He had to go back for her! There was no other choice.

It would take too long to go back the way he'd come. Frantically he searched the black mud for another trail of rocks to move along.

He'd gone several yards when he saw a figure emerge from the forest. Normally he wouldn't have been able to see the advancing person but the glow from The Ridge had cast an eerie, dancing illumination over the field.

And he saw, incredibly, Emma coming toward him! She'd spotted him and was waving.

No! She couldn't come out here! What was she thinking? "Stay put, Em!" he shouted. "I'll come to you!"

It seemed she couldn't hear him, because she kept coming forward.

"You crazy girl! What are you doing out here?" he muttered, leaping as quickly as he could from rock to rock.

Then he realized why she kept coming forward.

She saw him standing and thought it was safe. She couldn't tell that he was standing on a rock!

He shouted to her, "Em, hold up! It's not safe! I'm on a rock! Find a rock!"

Then she disappeared from sight, completely vanished!

"Emma!" he yelled as panic swept over him. She'd dropped into a mud-drenched bog and it had swallowed her whole.

He could no longer afford to search for rocks. He leaped into the mud, sinking instantly up to his knees. Pushing forward with all his strength, he waded through the thick sludge.

As he came closer he heard screaming, and new hope surged in him. She wasn't completely under! Her two arms flailed. "Hold still, Em," he called to her. "The more you struggle, the faster you'll sink."

Pulling his shirt over his head, he twirled it quickly into a line. Then he dropped to his stomach, inching forward on his elbows. When he thought he was close enough, he swung the shirt to her, holding tight to his end.

She grabbed it on the first throw.

He wrapped his end of the shirt tightly in his clenched fist. "Okay now, sug. Whatever happens, I've got my end and I won't let go no matter what. You don't let go either, hear me?"

He pulled on the shirt but he couldn't bring her straight up. Every time she rose a little, the mud sucked her back down.

Maybe this was similar to a riptide, he considered. When a riptide swept a person out to sea, it was best to swim from side to side instead of trying to head directly into shore. "Listen, Em, we're goin' to move sideways, just like crabs do. Stay cool and don't drop that line. We'll get you out."

She nodded as he began crawling to the side still clutching the shirt. He could see her neck, and soon her shoulders began to appear. "Hey, we're makin' progress," he cheered. "Ya, you right, it's workin'!"

The direction they were headed in was taking them closer to the road, but he didn't dare veer off. The bog she had sunken into was rising, and he couldn't risk taking her off its upward path.

Then she stopped moving. As much as he tugged, she was stuck.

"My skirt snagged!" she shouted.

"Can you slip it off?"

She shook her head. "I can't move my arms."

"Don't let go of the shirt," he said as he slipped into the mud beside her. "I'll unsnag you."

"Don't go!" she cried in a panic-filled voice.

"I'm a frog, remember? I love mud."

He filled his lungs until they felt full to bursting and then ducked his head under into the black world of ooze. He used her body as his guide, working his way down until he reached the end of her skirt. It was wrapped on a branch of some kind.

Moving in the mud was maddeningly slow. It closed in around him, seeping into his ears, his nose, pushing its way into his mouth. His breath was running out. What if he couldn't make his way up in time?

Her fingers began to clutch at him. Was she sinking? With a tug, the branch broke, setting her skirt free.

But how could he fight his way up without pulling her down?

He found footing on a ledge of stone beneath him and pushed against it. Grabbing her around the waist, he pushed up, hoping to keep her head above the muddy surface.

The rocky ledge continued, and he was able to keep on it and bring his nose and then his mouth above the mud.

With a whoosh, he breathed out and then sucked in fresh air.

He continued to hold her as they trudged out of the bog, heading for the road. He was shoulder high in mud, with Emma in his arms, when a brilliant light swept out of the darkness, blinding him.

He had no choice but to keep going toward it.

CHAPTER TWENTY-NINE
The Treasure

When Emma's eyes opened, she was no longer out in the dark night. Instead, she lay on a cot in a dimly lit hut. Her skin had become unnaturally tight and she could feel something gritty in her mouth.

Holding up her arm to the light, she saw it was completely caked with dried mud. Her entire body, from her hair to her boots, was covered in muck! She felt for her locket and discovered that it was, amazingly, still around her neck, though even it was also encrusted in the dry, flaking earth.

And then she remembered everything.

The fire. Her escape. Feeling overjoyed to see Jack in the fire's glow, moving out there on the field just when she'd given up on ever seeing him again. Feeling such a great need to get to him that she'd run out despite all she knew about the muddiness of the fields, all she'd come to warn him of; thinking that if he was standing, it must be safe.

Then the terrifying moment the mud sucked her down; the earth itself seemed to have become a hideous monster determined to consume her whole.

And then there he was beside her.

When everyone else had let her down, had gone away, had not come to get her, when the world itself had lost its mind—there he was.

He had gone down to the bottom of the muddy bog with only one purpose: to push her up.

What an idiot she'd been not to have seen him more clearly right away; how much he loved her, what a brave, large spirit he had. He'd never stopped trying to help the Allies, through his pain, his isolation, his capture; he'd never stopped trying. And all along he'd hidden these things from her; hidden them to keep her safe.

Truthfully, she knew she *had* seen it, but she'd fought against it. He seemed too strange to her, not the picture she had in mind of the person she would love.

A rueful laugh escaped her lips. Lloyd had been her image of the suitor she should have: status-minded, snobbish, two-faced Lloyd. So classically handsome and socially acceptable! How could she have been so wrong?

But where was Jack now?

Sitting up, she looked around the room. It was a simply furnished field office of some kind, with maps on the white walls—and a picture of Kaiser Wilhelm the Second. She recognized the German leader instantly from his photos in the newspapers.

Where *was* Jack?

Scrambling from the cot, she went to the window. There he was, outside, standing in front of a German soldier who was holding a pistol on him.

The soldier was going to shoot him!

Emma yanked the door open and ran to him, throwing her arms around his neck. Holding him tight, she kissed his mud-smeared lips with her own.

"Halt!" the soldier cried. "Stop that!"

"I love you," she whispered.

"I love you too, Em," he answered quietly.

"Stop or I will shoot you both right now!" the soldier insisted angrily.

Emma turned to him. As she did, she saw that her locket had slipped from her neck and fallen at her feet, its two halves sprung open. The locked compartment was finally open! Picking it up, she looked inside. Two deep red rubies lay nestled in the golden half sphere.

She stepped toward the soldier and thrust them at him. "Take these. They're very valuable. In exchange, just turn your back a moment and let us escape."

He laughed. "I don't need to bargain. I'll shoot you and then take them."

In a flash, she had them out of the locket and in her mouth. "I'll swallow them first." Slowly she walked backward to Jack. "Turn around and I'll leave them on this tree stump behind me," she said.

The soldier studied them with narrowed, suspicious eyes. "Put them down now."

Jack reached out for her hand and she took it. Together they backed up to the tree stump. Emma took the rubies from her mouth and set them down, keeping her hand on them until the soldier turned.

Together they raced down the hillside. The moon had come out, and they could see a river at the bottom of the hill; it was rushing fast, its wild current glistening silver.

Gunshots fired from on top of the hill. The soldier had come after them. A bullet rushed past Emma's face.

"Stay low. Keep running," Jack said, gripping her hand even tighter as they continued down the hill.

Another bullet whistled past.

Then, from atop the hill, came the clatter of machine gun fire.

Emma screamed just as they came to the riverbank. Something had hit her arm. Blood poured out. The searing pain was awful.

Guided by her scream, the next bullet grazed her forehead.

"Breathe deep," Jack said. Grabbing her beneath her armpit, he threw them both into the river.

CHAPTER THIRTY
Water Song

Jack swam in a river of silver ribbons that carried him along on their flowing strands, singing to him all along. The breezes skirting the shimmering white-caps carried music to his ears.

You belong to the river. You are prince of the water. You have won the heart of the one you love. Prince of the river. Prince of the water. Swim on. Swim on. Until you carry your love ashore. Swim on.

Obstructions filled the water, branches and clumps of matted leaves that had risen off the river-bank because the water was so high. It didn't matter to him. He pushed them aside easily. He felt light and strong, able to swim for miles, if he needed to.

Gripping Emma firmly across her chest and beneath her one arm, he kept her head above the water as he pulled with one arm and snapped his legs together in powerful scissor-kicks going forward.

The bullet that had grazed her head had knocked her unconscious. If he lost his grip on her, she would drown. But nothing would ever force him to let her go now.

She loved him. She had said it. She'd kissed him.

With one kiss she had turned him into a prince among men. Nothing else mattered now—not the Waifs' Home, not the hard days working on the docks, not the blistering afternoons mopping a deck, not the rat-infested trenches, not the burning gas in his eyes. None of it mattered anymore.

Her love had released him.

More than a kiss, she'd given him her tears. By trusting him, she'd made him realize how worthy of trust he had always been.

More than the kiss, she'd given him her vision of him. By seeing him clearly, she revealed all that he was inside—revealed it to him as well as to her. Her view of him became his view of himself, and he realized that the man she now saw was the one who had been there all along.

More than the kiss, her sacrifice made him see the essential beauty of her, the depth below the surface shine. When the locket split, it was as though her heart had opened to him.

But the kiss had been the magic token, the gesture of love, the mixing of energies that sealed the bond.

He was suddenly full of optimism about the future—their future together.

She loved him. She had said it. She'd kissed him.

The ribbons of silver that were sweeping him along slowly turned into strands of gold. Was he in Allied territory yet? It would be important to know, because the sun was rising and they would be easy to see, there in the water.

The golden, sun-flecked water began to sing him a new song. *Be gone from the river. Be gone, you prince of the water. The one you love needs magic from the land. Prince of the river. Prince of the water. Be gone. Be gone. Now carry your love ashore. Be gone.*

He knew this song was right. Emma needed to be out of the cold water. He had to see how bad her wounds were, how much blood she'd lost.

Just ahead, they came to a swirling eddy in the river. A tree had fallen into the water. Reaching out, he was able to grab hold of it to keep from moving with the rushing current.

Still holding tight to Emma, he dragged them both along the tree until he was able to sit in the shallow water. He pulled her up so that she was half on land and half in the shallow, watery banks because right then it was the best he could do; he needed a moment to recover.

He shivered in the cool morning air. Untying his shoes, he emptied the water from them, tied the laces together, and slung them around his neck. Pulling off his undershirt, he rang out the water from it before putting it back on. As much as he longed to collapse there awhile, he couldn't leave Emma in the bracingly cold river water.

He lifted her, carrying her to a dry patch of long grass and carefully laying her on it. Her blouse was torn and blood-soaked, exposing the place where the bullet had gashed her arm. He hoped it wasn't lodged inside the skin. He didn't think it was.

The river had washed them of mud and it had washed her wounds out too.

She'd been knocked out a long time.

Why wasn't she waking up?

Suddenly cold with fear, he put his thumb on her jugular vein.

He didn't feel a pulse. He put his hand on her heart.

"Aw, c'mon, Em, give me something," he urged, fighting panic.

Nothing.

He checked her mouth to make sure she hadn't swallowed anything in the river that was stopping her from breathing. No. "Em, wake up!" he shouted, shaking her.

Kneeling beside her, he thumped her heart hard with his fist. He thought he heard the sound of bone cracking. He drew back, horrified by what he'd done, but then forced himself to keep on with it, remembering the training he'd received in the army.

He threw all his weight onto her, pressing with both his palms, pumping them, trying to force her heart to start beating once again.

She couldn't leave him now. She loved him. She'd said it. She'd kissed him.

Throwing his head back, he began to sing a

healing song his mother had taught him. She'd learned it from her great-grandmother, a Natchez medicine woman. He'd heard her sing it, asking the Great Spirit for help. He threw his head back and sang the song in a plaintive, heartfelt wail as he pumped at Emma's heart.

Finally he felt it—just a blip, at first. Then stronger. Her heart was pumping on its own.

Collapsing at her side, his own heart pounding wildly, he stayed there feeling his heartbeat gradually normalize. She turned her head to him and blinked.

He brushed some wet hair from her forehead.

"Are we alive?" she asked him, her voice a rasp.

He smiled softly back at her. "I think so, Em. But maybe we'd better go ask the queen."

The next day was clear with rolling white clouds, and though they slept through most of it, they were aware that poppies and daffodils were everywhere, growing wild all around. He stayed up long enough to find berries and dandelion greens for a meal. Though it didn't quite quell the ache of hunger, it was enough to keep them alive. And dandelion greens worked as a blood purifier. They'd help her fight infection.

He did the best he could to tend her wounds, glad to find a balsam fir tree with some sap still in a cut in its bark. He got as much of the sap as he could and smeared it over the cuts, knowing it would help heal.

While she slept, he built them a raft, lashing

branches together with his shoelaces, unraveled thread from his socks, and strips torn from his pants and the bottom of her under slip. As the sun set, he pushed the raft to the riverbank and carried Emma to it, settling her as comfortably as he could before pushing off with a thick fallen branch.

The river was filled to overflowing from all the rain and rushed along quickly, carrying them, he calculated, closer to the port town of Dunkirk. The last he knew, the Allies still held Dunkirk and they would be safe there.

"How are you doin', Em?" he asked her as she lay on the raft.

"Tired. It hurts when I try to turn." Her voice lacked strength and she was pale; it worried him.

"You sleep, then," he advised, arranging his jacket over her like a blanket. "The river will carry us."

Reaching out, she put her hand in his, letting sleep take her once more. The sunset darkened, and while the moon rose, he held her hand, watching the moonlit scenery go by. It was an incredibly beautiful country. It seemed all wrong that it should be so torn apart by this war.

When he'd traveled north up the Mississippi he'd later gone up the Ohio River by raft. It was gorgeous country too, but back then he hadn't had the eyes to appreciate it. He'd only cared about getting to his destination. But now the natural richness all around overwhelmed him. All that he'd seen of the war had changed him.

As he sat guard beside her sleeping figure, he understood for the first time that it was not only the war that had made him alive as never before to the beauty of the world; his love for Emma had re-created him. The love she returned to him had done it too. Their love for each other had worked the magic.

He'd drifted off to sleep on the raft beside Emma but awoke with a start. In the dawn's first light he could make out buildings lining the shore: shops, a church, taverns, bakeries; two-story establishments of all kinds. Back in the trees were houses. He'd stopped at Dunkirk one night when he first came over from England. He recognized right away that the river was taking them into Dunkirk's waterfront. "Em, wake up, sug. We made it."

She stirred, propping up sleepily onto her elbows and smiling.

The chugging engine of an approaching boat made them look over to it. Four British soldiers stood in the boat's stern with their rifles slung across their backs. Jack waved to them, sweeping his arms wide.

Two of the soldiers readied their rifles, pointing them at Jack as the boat pulled alongside the raft. "It's all right sir, I know this fellow," one of the soldiers said.

"Kid!" Jack cried happily.

"He's with the British Fourth Army, sir," the Kid

continued to tell his captain. "He saved my life when we were both captured by the Germans."

Jack saluted the captain. "Welcome home, soldier," the officer replied, returning the salute.

"My friend here, Miss Emma Winthrop, is injured and needs care right away," Jack told the captain. "I request help in lifting her onto your boat and getting her to a hospital."

Kid was the first one down to help. Together, he and Jack got Emma onto the boat. "I have information regarding the upcoming Allied advance," Jack told the captain.

"How did you know about that?" the captain asked.

"I heard about it from the Germans."

"Let's get ashore and hear what you have to say right away," the captain said.

Jack sat beside Emma, who had been laid inside the boat's small cabin. He took her hand, squeezing it gently.

"Are we okay now?" she asked, gazing up at him.

"We are right as rain, Em," he replied.

EPILOGUE
London, November 1918

Emma stepped off the ship in Dover. She hadn't been back in England in over a year, not since she signed up to join the U.S. Army Signal Corps and had gone back to the Western Front in France to help with the war effort.

The Americans had joined the war in 1917 and formed the Signal Corps, recruiting women who were fluent in English and French to work the switchboards and relay messages between the advancing American, English, Canadian, and French troops.

How ironic, she'd written in one of her many letters to Jack. *You're serving in the British army and I'm in an American unit with other women who are, for the most part, Americans. It doesn't matter, though; we're all on the same side. The conditions are very hard here though I am sure they are worse for you. We sit at our switchboards for long hours and relay messages, often having to interpret. We even have to know about military terms and weaponry in order to make sure our interpretations are understandable. Helmets and gas masks hang behind our chairs and make me think of you and all you are going through. How I long to see you again.*

They were able to see each other for a day in Paris in 1917. It was July 6, her nineteenth birthday! The greatest birthday gift she could imagine was being there and sitting in a café on the Champs-Élysée with him. When it was time to read the menu, he took out a pair of wire-rimmed glasses and hooked them on. "The eyes never fully came back the way they were," he explained. "I suppose I got off easy, all things considered."

"I like the way they look," she assured him sincerely. He looked so tired, though. The endless fighting was taking such a toll on him. He was thin and pale.

"It can't go on forever, Em," he'd said that day as he kissed her good-bye outside the café; but she'd begun to wonder if maybe it could. "When this is over, I'll come find you wherever you are," he promised.

"That might not be possible," she pointed out.

"Leave it to me," he'd assured her. She'd come to trust him completely. If he said he'd find her, he would.

Finally, though, on November 11, the war ended. It took almost two weeks more before she could get to Calais and get a boat across the channel to Dover Beach. In the two weeks, she kept searching for him among the lines of moving troops plodding home, hoping for a message or for his sudden appearance.

She kept pushing the thought out of her mind that he might be dead.

He couldn't be dead.

It would be more than she could stand if he was dead. And yet so many were.

The crowd disembarking from the boat had begun to disperse as their friends and relatives arrived to pick them up. She'd sent her father a telegram telling him that she had a friend who would bring her home, as she wasn't sure exactly when she would be arriving. Once she'd booked passage on the boat, she'd sent one telegram after another to the Fourth Army trying to tell Jack where she was. Every day she'd gone to the telegram office in Calais hoping for a response, but none ever came.

She spied a stand of motorized taxi cabs over by the tariff house. When she'd left, horse carriages were still in use. Though she'd seen motorized ambulances in the war, the motor cabs reminded her too much of the armored tanks both sides had begun using toward the end and she didn't welcome the thought of getting into one.

It didn't appear that she had much other choice.

With a sigh, she began walking toward the stand. She was nearly to the taxi when someone stepped into her path. "Welcome home, Em."

Emma blinked hard, not sure at first that he was real. Then he smiled at her and her sense of unreality gave way to a wave of nearly overwhelming joy. Throwing herself into his arms, she showered him with kisses, holding him tight as if to make sure he'd never go away again. Tears of happiness flooded her eyes.

"Hey, now, no crying," he said softly.

She wiped her eyes. "It's all right," she assured him. "I'm just so glad to see you—so glad."

"I know. Me too," he replied, and she saw a glint of wetness in his eyes, as well. He enfolded her in his arms, an embrace she never wanted to end.

Only afterward did she notice the medal on his chest. It was a bar from which hung a gold cross with a round middle. In the golden round center of the cross a crowned lion posed proudly with the words FOR VALOUR underneath.

"The Victoria Cross!" she cried. It was England's highest honor for gallantry in the face of the enemy. "It's wonderful, but what did you do to get this? I'm so glad I wasn't there to see it."

He laughed his familiar, raspy chuckle. "But you *were* there, Em, every step of the way."

"I was?"

"I got this for crossing enemy lines to warn the Allies that the Germans already knew the timing of the advance they'd planned. They figured we saved a lot of lives by doing that. By rights, you should have one of these too, so let's say we share it."

She entwined her fingers through his and laid her head on his shoulder, so happy that he'd come back to her, healthy and strong, with his love for her still alive in his heart.

About the Author

SUZANNE WEYN is also the author of *The Night Dance*, a retelling of the Grimms' fairytale "The Twelve Dancing Princesses," intertwined with Arthurian legends. Her other young-adult novels include the romantic comedy *South Beach Sizzle*, written with Diana Gonzalez. Suzanne's science-fiction thriller for young adults, *The Bar Code Tattoo*, was selected by the American Library Association as a 2005 Quick Pick for Reluctant Young Adult Readers. *The Bar Code Rebellion* is the sequel.